LIA ANDERSON
DOG PARK MYSTERIES

Muddy Mouth

Muddy Mouth

A Dog Park Mystery

C. A. Newsome

TWO PUP
PRESS

MUDDY MOUTH

Chewy by Carol Ann Newsome
Cover design by Elizabeth Mackey
Copyright © 2016 by Carol Ann Newsome

ISBN-13: 978-0-9963742-4-8

Published by Two Pup Press
1836 Bruce Avenue
Cincinnati, Ohio 45223

For librarians everywhere.
You are society's equalizers.

Cast of Characters
(and their dogs)

Featuring

Lia Anderson, (Honey and Chewy)
Detective Peter Dourson (Viola)

The Missing Author

Leroy Eberschlag/Lucas Cross, author
Dorothy Eberschlag, Leroy's mother, Debby's sister
Citrine/Cheryl Baremore, artist and blogger
Koi, fictional covert operative
Colt Savage, fictional investigator
George Wier, author and AustinCon organizer
Russell Blake, author
Nick Russell, author

Knot Only Knitting, AKA Fiber and Snark

Sarah Schellenger, Northside Branch Librarian
Carol Cohn, semi-retired bookkeeper
Debby Carrico, Elmwood Branch Librarian
Cecilie Watkins, founder of SCOOP
Alice Emons, Architect
Duane Adams, Sarah's husband, A sound engineer
Jerry Carrico, Debby's husband, owner of an automotive bodyshop
Bill Watkins, Cecilie's husband
Tom Emons, Alice's husband

Mount Airy Dog Park
Bailey Hughes (Kita)
Jim McDonald (Fleece)
Bonnie (Chester)
Jose Mitsch (Sophie)
Terry Dunn (Jackson and Napa)
Steve Reams (Penny)
Renee Solomon (Dakini)

District 5
Captain Bill Roller, current commander
Captain Ann Parker, incoming commander
Detective Brent Davis, Peter's partner
Detective Cynth McFadden, electronic investigator
Officer Cal Hinkle
Officer Paul Brainard
Detective Hodgkins AKA Heckle
Detective Jarvis AKA Jeckle

Everyone Else
Alma, Peter's octogenarian neighbor
Ruth Peltier, Peter's recently deceased neighbor
Edward, Twin Towers resident
Trees, AKA John Morgan, hacker and Bailey's long-distance beau
Paul Ravenscraft, musician, massage therapist and non-denominational minister
Asia, Lia's therapist

Prologue

From the *Cincinnati Enquirer*:

Author Vanishes

AUSTIN, TX - In a scenario right out of one of his books, best selling author Lucas Cross vanished in the early hours of June 11th from AustinCon, a convention of self-published authors taking place this weekend at the Hyatt Regency Hotel. Cross' entourage first realized he was missing when he failed to appear for an author panel Saturday morning. He was last seen at a party for the panel held in a suite tenanted by best-selling author Russell Blake.

Witnesses recalled seeing Cross in an inebriated state at 11 P.M. No one remembered seeing him leave. According to Austin Police, signs of a disturbance in the hotel basement suggest Cross did not leave the hotel voluntarily.

Cross, a Cincinnati writer whose real name is Leroy Eberschlag, attended the convention accompanied by an aunt, Debby Carrico, along with his accountant and his editorial team, none of whom attended the party. Carrico appeared at a press conference held by Austin Police, making a tearful plea for the safe return of her nephew.

Chapter 1

Friday, June 17

"That was fun, but I still don't get his appeal." Lia shoved the push bar on the rear door of the Esquire Theater, exiting into the night. She was a slender woman, five-nine with moss-green eyes and elegant cheekbones. Her streaky chestnut hair piled messily on her head as a concession to 80% humidity. This was date night, so she'd worn a boho peasant blouse over a multi-patterned maxi skirt instead of her usual khaki shorts and paint splattered tee shirt.

She and her companion, Detective Peter Dourson, preferred the back way out. The rehabbed Art Deco movie house had a tiny lobby that was always crowded at night. Lia paused in the alley, feeling the sultry night breeze against her face. "I suspect I'll enjoy being outside for exactly five minutes - until it starts feeling clammy."

Peter traced the tips of his fingers down her spine and snugged a proprietary hand at her waist. "It's a good thing we'll be in the car by then."

They emerged from the alley into the Friday night throngs on Ludlow Avenue, illuminated by the vintage gaslights that were the hallmark of the trendy Cincinnati neighborhood. Peter took Lia's hand as he forced a path through the milling crowd in front of the theater.

Self-reliant all her life by necessity, Lia was still adjusting to Peter's protective ways. Sometimes when he led her like this it made her feel like a child and she had to resist a perverse urge to pull her hand away. The fault, she knew, was with her. On date nights, she surrendered to Peter's gentlemanly manners, consciously choosing to enjoy them.

It wasn't much of a hardship. Tall and lean, with mink-brown hair that fell into eyes the deep blue of twilight, Peter was attractive more than handsome. She found she liked that about him. She'd had enough of handsome men.

When she'd first met the detective, she hadn't thought he was her type. Growing up in the far reaches of Kentucky groomed him for an earlier era of gentle chauvinism that sometimes made him seem much older, though at 34, he was only one year her senior. More observant than gregarious, she'd thought his personality as bland as his khakis and regulation polos. Not the guy for an artist.

Caught up in the death of her then-boyfriend, she hadn't noticed the strength in his lean frame and the humor in his eyes. She'd only had to dip her toe in to discover currents running powerfully swift and deep in Peter.

A dreadlocked sax player moaned a bluesy riff on the next corner, competing with a trio of African drummers a block away. Traffic slowed to avoid jay walkers. Light spilled out of stylish boutiques, still open to lure window shoppers on their way to or from dinner in one of the many restaurants.

The saxophone player had already amassed a healthy pile of bills in his instrument case, likely a result of snaring the corner by Graeter's Ice Cream Parlor and Bakery, the most crowded corner in the Gaslight District of Clifton. Patrons poured onto the street, tongues flashing to catch the ice cream dripping down their sugar cones. Some made their way to the benches lining Telford Avenue, some were headed for the plaza overlooking the parking lot, and others lingered around the busker.

"Ice cream?" Peter asked.

"You get some if you want. I'm trying to be good. Milk products are off my diet."

Peter's sweet tooth mourned in silence. "Along with popcorn, pizza, and nachos. If the line wasn't so long, I'd grab three dips of raspberry chocolate chip so you'd have to watch me eat it."

"Cruel man. Wheat and corn are bad for type O's. Dr. D'Adamo says so." She ignored his rolling eyes and bumped his hip. "If I don't notice more energy after 90 days, I'll ditch the diet and treat you to Dewey's every night for a week. The light's green, let's go."

The other side of the street was deserted. They took a shortcut, passing into a narrow alley between Om Cafe and a small shop that was forever changing identities, both closed. Lia thought the brick-lined darkness a suitable epilogue to an evening watching classic noir cinema.

"So you won't be fantasizing about Bogie tonight?" Peter asked.

"Nope."

"What's not to like?"

"His head is shaped funny, it looks like he has no neck, and he's too aggressive for my taste," Lia said.

"That's not aggression, it's manliness," Peter said.

"It's manly to slap Peter Lorre over and over? The man was wearing a white suit and smelled like gardenias. It was like kicking a poodle." Lia gave him an incredulous look.

"Bogie is the ultimate romantic. I thought women loved him."

"He sneers at Mary Astor and calls her a liar about twenty times. Then he tells her he can't trust her. He grabs her face and mashes his mouth into hers in the worst screen kiss ever, and implies the only way he'll stick with her is if she sleeps with him. What about that is supposed to make me swoon?"

Peter took Lia by the shoulders and pressed her against the wall. He caged her face with his forearms and leaned in close, nuzzling her neck, sending shivers through her body.

"You don't like masterful men?"

Lia gasped as his breath feathered her ear. "Mastery..."

Peter traced one index finger along her hairline, wrapping it in a strand of hair and giving it a gentle tug.

Lis struggled to remember her point. "... implies finesse...."

He kissed her jaw.

"...I saw no finesse in that kiss."

"Maybe," Peter murmured as he kissed his way from her jaw to her mouth, "he ... was overcome ... with passion." He pressed a knee between her legs as he took her face in both hands, his mouth hovering over hers while his thumbs drew circles on her temples. He held her eyes for a long moment, warm breath feathering between them.

A woman screamed.

Peter bolted for the end of the alley, the pounding of his feet echoing off the buildings. Lia pushed herself away from the wall and followed. By the time she emerged onto the back lot of Om Cafe, Peter was hurtling down the steps that led to the parking lot, taking three at a time.

"Did you see him? Did you see him?" The woman's voice was hysterical.

"Are you hurt?" Peter's voice drifted up the steps.

"That man, is he still there?"

"What man?"

"He pushed me. He was there, at the top of the steps. I thought he was going to come down and kill me!"

Peter craned his neck, catching Lia's eye. She shook her head. Whoever had been there was gone. She grabbed the steel handrail and made her way down the long, concrete steps as Peter questioned the woman.

"He's gone," Peter told her. "What did he look like?... Where are you hurt?"

The woman's voice, calmer now, was too faint for Lia to make out as she answered Peter's questions.

The tiny woman sat on the asphalt, surrounded by her scattered belongings. Peter stooped beside her, his arm behind her back. A disheveled puff of red hair hovered above oversized glasses perched on a small nose. A scrape on her forehead oozed. The pale face, pinched in pain, was familiar.

"Carol? Carol Cohn?"

7

Carol looked up. "Do I know you?"

"Lia Anderson. Sarah's friend. She hired me to build your parade float."

Carol blinked. "Right. Forgive me, I'm distracted. Did you see him? A tall man in a dark hoodie?"

"I didn't see anyone," Lia said. "He must have ducked around one of the buildings."

"Stay with her for a minute. I need to call this in," Peter said.

Lia crouched on the asphalt while Peter stood up and turned his back. Carol's stockings were shredded and one shoe was missing. Her left ankle ballooned below a calf covered in road rash.

"We should call you an ambulance."

"No ... no. If you can just drive me to Good Sam and help me to the emergency room, I can call Sarah from there. I'm sure she and Duane can pick me up and get my car."

"Are you sure? Your ankle looks painful."

"Not as painful as the cost of an ambulance, if my insurance decides not to cover it." Carol set her mouth in a determined line.

Lia decided not to press the point. Good Samaritan was less than a quarter mile away. An ambulance was silly, if Carol felt well enough to argue about it. Of course, Carol was a semi-retired accountant. Pain was no match for a lifetime of penny pinching.

Peter knelt beside them. "Your description is not much to go on. They're routing patrol cars to this area, but they may not be able to find him unless he attacks someone else. Still, it's worth a shot."

"Peter, she doesn't want an ambulance. Can we take her up to Good Sam?"

"Sure. I'll pull the car around. Mrs. Cohn, can you sit here while Lia gathers your things? Will you be okay?"

"You won't go far, will you?" Carol looked anxiously at Lia.

Lia stroked her shoulder. "I'll be less than 20 feet away. Where did you lose your shoe? Do you know?"

"It fell off on the steps somewhere. Maybe it's in the weeds. I hope you can find it. This is my favorite pair of walking shoes." She blinked back tears as she examined the scraped leather. Lia's own eyes watered as she watched the woman's misery.

Using her phone as a flashlight, Lia found the shoe in a clump of chicory growing out of a pile of broken brick half way up the steep bank. She shook her head, wondering how fast Carol fell to send her shoe that far, and how she managed to escape worse injury.

Lia shook her head at the trash littering the bank. Despite the merchants association's best efforts, garbage from the UDF convenience store around the corner still made its way to the parking lot along with other forms of detritus.

Carol's classic handbag—in beige leather that matched her StrideRite walking shoes—lay next to a mess of Middle Eastern food spilling out of a torn paper bag. While Carol cradled the shoe like a baby, Lia righted the purse and brushed bits of tabouli off the side, then set out to retrieve the river of change, coupons and balled up tissues which belched across the pavement, using the few clean napkins from Carol's take-out dinner to wipe humus off of the coins. She stuffed what trash she could into

9

the bag to throw away, but there was nothing she could do about the pile of food.

She picked up a lipstick and an engraved keychain. The light from her phone glinted on something in the weeds. It turned out to be the needle of a syringe. Probably belonged to the guy who shoved Carol. It made sense that a drug addict would mug someone. *At least he didn't have a chance to grab her wallet after he shoved her down the steps.*

The headlights of Peter's Ford explorer cast harsh shadows that panned across the scene as he pulled up. Carol looked even more vulnerable, sitting on the pavement in a pool of light. He left the SUV running as he picked Carol up and gently placed her in the passenger seat. Lia climbed in the back.

"I called Good Sam," Peter said. "They'll have someone meet us at the door with a wheelchair. You're getting curb service because of the assault. An officer will meet you there to take your statement and document your injuries."

Carol sniffed. She set the shoe that no longer fit her swollen foot in her lap and dug a tissue out of her purse. She dabbed delicately at her eyes and nose. "I don't know what I would have done if you hadn't come along. I've lived here all my life. Ludlow has always been so safe, I don't know what to think. You've been so kind."

"It's the least we could do, Mrs. Cohn." Peter dug a business card out of his pocket and handed it to her. She clutched it to her breast like an autograph from Harrison Ford. "The officer will give you contact information, but if you have any problems, you can call me."

"Next time I get a yen for baba ganooj after dark, I'm just going to ignore it." A corner of her mouth quirked bravely.

"Maybe bring a friend, and take the steps off the plaza. They're better lit, and not so isolated."

"Never had to worry about it before," Carol grumbled.

"No, ma'am."

An officer waited at the ER entrance with an attendant and a wheelchair. Lia recognized Cal Hinkle by his haystack of blonde hair.

"I've got it now, Detective Dourson. Ma'am, I'm Officer Hinkle." He indicated the man in scrubs. "This is Harold. He's going to help you to that wheelchair and we're going to take care of you." He nodded to Peter and Lia, then turned his attention to Carol.

Lia climbed into the front seat. She turned around to watch the tiny procession as Peter drove away.

"What do you supposed happened?"

Peter shrugged. "Some thug, probably a meth head or heroin addict, shoved her down the steps. He heard me coming so he ran off before he could grab her purse. It's fairly typical."

"Don't purse snatchers usually grab the purse first, then shove?"

"He's new to crime and hasn't developed his technique? If that's the case, there's a good chance he'll get picked up sooner than later."

"I hope it happens before anyone else gets hurt. Carol could have been killed. I'm glad they sent Cal to interview her. He's very reassuring."

"Older women love him," Peter said. "It's his super power."

"It's the scrubbed freckles. They're irresistible."

"Not to you, I hope." He reached over and squeezed her thigh.

"Well..."

"If you're immune to Humphrey Bogart..."

"That's different. He was mean."

"*Maltese Falcon* was early in his career. We'll watch *Casablanca* next time, or one of his films with Lauren Bacall. You'll see a different side to him."

"Oh?"

"He and Lauren Bacall fell in love on the set of *To Have and to Have Not*, but he was married to a violent alcoholic. They carried on a hot affair for years. It shows on the screen."

"Really?" Lia drew the word out.

"Hotter than Brad Pitt and Angelina Jolie."

"I never much cared for either of them."

"You're a hard woman to please, Ms. Anderson."

"Oh, I don't know about that." Lia combed her fingers through the hair hanging over Peter's collar and wished cars still came with bench seats. "You please me quite well, Detective Dourson."

Peter caught her hand and kissed her fingers. "Not yet, but we'll see about that.

Chapter 2

Saturday, June 18

Lia took a sip of her take-out coffee before setting the cup on the roof of her car. She looked out over Mount Airy Dog Park, noting that for once, she did not enjoy the long shadows cast by the rising sun. She opened the rear door of her ancient Volvo. Her miniature schnauzer, Chewy, bounced to her side while Honey, a golden retriever, exited the car with dignity. *I'm not ready for this. No more late nights with Peter until after the parade.* She juggled their leashes with her coffee cup, then headed for the inclined service road leading to the dog park entrance.

The Northside Fourth of July Parade was a community tradition and a tribute to the neighborhood's reputation as diverse, funky and creative. Anyone could propose an entry. This year, Lia and her dog park friends were performing routines with their dogs. Lia was also building a float for Lucas Cross, AKA Leroy Eberschlag. The float featured a giant Browning Buckmark .22 pistol to celebrate Cross' soon-to-be-released *Savage Gun*.

"Best behavior, Little Man," Lia admonished Chewy, who was currently dragging her up the road.

"Please pretend you remember something from our last eight sessions." Chewy continued to lunge on his leash like a hooked bass. Lia turned to Honey. "As for you, Missy, no laughing."

Honey looked back at her mistress with an expression that seemed to say, "Me? Laugh? How could you think such a thing?" She stopped and ducked her head to sniff at Heavens-knew-what, telegraphing hurt as she dug in her paws. Chewy continued his ascent.

Lia stood, arms outstretched, unable to move in either direction. A furry boulder goosed Lia's rear. She yelped.

"Sophie, can't you see her hands are full?" Jose Mitsch called to the mastiff now leaning against Lia's side, seeking attention. "Lia will pet you later." Jose was a tall man, with an erect carriage that made Lia think he had been in the military or had played football. But an ancient, home-made tattoo of his name on his knuckles and a Fu Manchu mustache hinted at biker origins. She'd never asked. She knew the maintenance supervisor was endlessly kind to animals and could build or repair anything.

He overtook Lia, who was still caught in limbo between her dogs. "I'll take Chewy off your hands for you."

"Thanks, Jose," Lia said, handing over the leash. Sophie bent her massive head to sniff Chewy's nose and the pair ambled ahead. Honey appeared at Lia's side as if her snit had never happened. Instead, she looked up at Lia, as if to say, "Well, what are you waiting for?"

Lia curbed a sigh. Nothing like Chewy getting attention to bring Honey front and center. She lengthened her stride to catch up with Jose. Ironically, Chewy had now stopped and was peeing on the park fence.

"The float is coming along great. I can't thank you enough for helping with the armature."

"No problemo. You know what they say about men and their toys."

What is that?"

"The only thing better than a gun is a bigger gun." he winked. "And that gun is big enough to take out passing satellites. I can now say I helped build the biggest replica of a Browning Buckmark ever made. We oughta enter it in the *Guinness Book of World Records*. It'll be somethin' rolling down Hamilton Avenue on the fourth. You know what would be really cool?"

What's that?"

"We should fix it so it shoots a person out, and there's a net rolling behind to catch him."

Lia rolled her eyes. "Sure Jose. You get with Jim and figure out how to make that happen. Are you volunteering to be the human projectile?"

"Oh, man, that would be great. Is the float still in the parade, with Leroy missing?"

"I assume so. He may be missing, but his books are still for sale. Sarah's meeting me at the garage this afternoon. I'll find out more when I see her."

"Building a float, training Chewy to do dance routines, you're gonna be all over this parade."

They rounded a curve that brought them up to a brick and concrete picnic shelter with attached restrooms. The shelter split the dog park into two separate enclosures that together, ran the length of the six acre ridge comprising the former Highpoint picnic area. The pair of remaining picnic tables had been shoved out of the way to make room for an ad hoc training ring. A half-dozen park regulars stood chatting while their dogs mingled, tangling leads.

Chewy surged sideways, shooting down the path beside the smaller enclosure.

"What the hell happened?" Jose asked, Chewy's leash dangling from his hand.

"Clasp failure," Lia announced, pressing Honey's leash into Jose's hand in exchange for Chewy's as she dashed after the escaping dog.

Lia cursed mentally. *Why can't he be like Viola?* Peter's dog, Viola, liked to run free, but she always stayed close to other dogs and wouldn't run off on her own. It was easy to catch her. Chewy liked to follow his nose. He rarely paid attention to where he was going, so you couldn't count on him to find his way back. Chances were good he'd patrol the outside of the fence. If she cut him off from the inside of the park, his recapture might be quick. Thank God she'd brought treats for today's training.

Lia navigated the entry corral, then paused, scanning the fence line. Sure enough, Chewy had turned at the far end of the enclosure and was trotting along the back side. Lia crossed the park, aiming for a spot that would be well ahead of Chewy when he made the second turn. The goal was for Chewy to come to her on his ramble. If she ran up to him, it would start a game of chase. Who knew where that would end?

By the time Chewy met up with Lia, he'd forgotten he was an escapee and was perfectly content to follow her back around to the gate as long as she fed the occasional treat through the fence. She checked her exasperation.

Chewy wouldn't understand it, and the only impact it would have on him would be negative.

Renee Solomon, Lia's art patron and trainer of the Mount Airy Dog Stars by universal agreement, waited with Jose at the beginning of the path. She was a petite brunette who wore her chin-length hair, which was practically a mandate in Cincinnati, in non-mandated, spiraling curls. Rigorous exercise and high-dollar grooming kept her looking much younger than her forty-odd years. Her exceptionally well-kept appearance was exceeded only by that of her gorgeous champion collie, Dakini. Only Renee's middle-class roots and cheerful good nature kept everyone from being demoralized by their combined perfection.

"What happened?" Renee asked.

"Either the clasp failed, or he's channeling Houdini. This is the third time in a month."

Renee examined Chewy's leash. "You've got a lobster-claw clasp. It should not happen."

"And yet it does."

"You might want to try a slip lead like Dakini's." Renee leaned over and parted Dakini's abundant mane to reveal the leash, which was rolled leather with a loop created by feeding the leash through a brass ring stitched into the end. "It's all one piece, so Chewy wouldn't be able to get out of it, not unless you forget to adjust the leather slide that keeps the loop from opening up. All show dogs use them. I suggest a four foot lead, at least to start with. If you get one, I'll show you how to use it properly."

Dollar signs tugged on Lia's conscience as she considered the cost of a leather lead. "This looks like a choke collar. I thought choke collars were bad."

"It's dangerous to leave a choke collar on a dog while it's unsupervised, or when it's playing with other dogs. And you should never use a slip lead or a choke collar on a dog that's less than 18 months old because their neck bones are still forming. Slip leads allow you to give an immediate, gentle correction to a dog. But your problem is bigger than the leash. I suspect you need to spend more time with Chewy on fundamental obedience, if you had to lure him back with treats."

Lia sighed. "I was working two jobs and starting my own business when Chewy showed up. I taught him the basics, but he hasn't had as much training as Honey did. I hoped to use the parade as an opportunity to fix that. He's really good. He just gets distracted."

Renee frowned. "Be sure to fill your left pocket with treats before the parade. It will help keep him focused on you."

"Why the left?"

"It's closest to his nose. Try it out on your next practice session. You may need to carry a treat in your left hand, if it isn't enough. Be sure to exercise him before training sessions." She looked at her watch. "We'd better get started."

They rejoined the group in the pavilion. Lia's best friend, Bailey, leaned over a boombox. The lanky woman with her swing of red hair was tailed by an equally lanky bloodhound named Kita.

"Didn't boom boxes go out with big hair?" Lia asked while Honey and Kita sniffed noses. "What do we need those for?"

Bailey shrugged "Renee suggested it. We'll have insane amounts of noise at the parade, and it's time to get the dogs used to it. It's not enough to have the dogs know the routine, they need to be able to do it with drums and sirens, plus the occasional firecracker. I have another boom box that we can put on the outside wall."

"But boom boxes?"

Bailey shrugged. "They cost next to nothing at Saint Vincent de Paul, and I have tons of old cassettes. I even have some John Philip Sousa marches from my brother's high school band days."

"If that doesn't do it, nothing will."

"I also pulled the soundtrack off a YouTube video of the parade from a couple years ago. It includes African American drum core music and fire truck sirens."

"Even better," Renee said, joining them.

"They came with remotes," Bailey said, handing the black, plastic oblongs to Renee. "So you can adjust the volume while we're working."

"The dogs will either be ready for a Zen monastery or the booby hatch when we're done with them." Renee turned to the group. "Okay everyone, take your positions."

Lia put Honey into a down-stay by the shelter wall and took her place next to Jose and Sophie, with Chewy at her left. They and their dogs formed one side of a large square. On her right, Jim McDonald and his lady-friend Bonnie made up a side with Fleece and Chester. Renee and Terry made up the third side with Dakini and Jackson, while Bailey and Terry's roommate, Steve, completed the square with their dogs, Kita and Penny.

Renee turned on one boom box at low volume, then started the group with some basic sit-stays, heeling, and returns. When everyone was warmed up, she took them through a weaving routine, with the women circling clockwise and the men headed in the other direction. The formation morphed through several variations until everyone met in the center and put their dogs into a down-stay, walked to the end of their leads, then signaled the dogs to heel. The dogs approached their owners on the right, circled behind them, then sat at their left side.

"Great job!" Renee said. "Okay, I'd like to try a new routine with some square dance moves. Let's get back to our original positions."

Jackson and Chester got their leashes hung up during a do-si-do. The two dogs took this opportunity to run around Terry and Bonnie in circles for a may-pole effect. Renee left Dakini with a snappy "stay" hand signal to untangle the mess while everyone else fell into hysterical laughter.

Order restored, Renee tried an allemande, which had the dogs running into each other in the center of the formation. She widened the square and tried again, with better results. After a few more foul ups, Renee returned the group to walking their dogs at heel in an evenly spaced square around the pavilion. She had steadily raised the volume of the boom boxes during the course of their practice. Now a fire truck siren blasted the pavilion. All the dogs stopped, howling in unison. Renee turned off the music and the howls died away, silence ringing in Lia's ears.

"I'll have to make sure we're nowhere near the trucks when we're marching," she said. "I think it's time to call it quits for today. Anyone have any thoughts about what we have so far?"

"I think we need to rearrange the dogs," Bonnie said. "Every time we start to heel, Chester tries to run up Fleece's tail and sniff her privates. I don't think that's proper in front of children. "

"He does that to her all the time at home," Jim said. "Why are you saying something now?"

"I didn't think he'd do it in public," Bonnie said.

"He's a dog. He doesn't care who's watching," Jim said.

"Chester is a pervert. Don't you know that he likes to sniff tail?" Terry asked.

"I've never been with him around so many dogs at one time," Bonnie said.

"You'd know it if you came with me in the mornings," Jim grumbled.

"We're talking about a parade," Bonnie said. "I don't think children should see that."

"They might as well get used to it. It's normal dog behavior and they're going to see it for the rest of their lives," said Jim.

"Bonnie," Renee interrupted, "Since we change directions during the routine, Chester is going to be behind Fleece at some point, unless you'd like to partner with someone else?"

"No, I don't want that," Bonnie said.

"The best thing to do is to spend more time heeling with Chester at home, so that he gets used to staying beside you. Have you been practicing?"

Bonnie's eyes slid away.

"Ten minutes a day will do wonders. Even five will help. Maybe you and Jim can train together. Dogs learn from each other."

"Do you think we have too many flourishes?" Lia asked, changing the subject. "I'm worried the dogs are going to get confused and mess up during the parade."

"This is Northside," Steve said. "Consider it comic relief."

"If we know the routines and signal our dogs properly, everything will be fine," Renee said. "The dogs are not learning the routines as much as they are learning to follow you. Consistency is key. Also, as they get used to working with distractions, their focus will improve and the behaviors we saw today are going to go away. Keep training them to heel when we aren't practicing. Be sure to include u-turns and circles going in both directions. Don't forget music, as loud as you can."

"I think we need costumes for the dogs," Bailey said. "Something cute, don't you think?"

"I got a bunch of bungee cords and zip ties down at the shop," Jose said. "Maybe we can do something with them."

"Bungee cords and zip ties? Yeah that will work," Steve cracked. "We can do '50 shades of Rover' for our theme."

"I know an easy way to make inexpensive tutus," Lia said. "And the same technique can be used to make ruffs. What do you think? Tutus for the girls and ruffs for the boys?"

"As long as we're talking about dogs, not handlers," said Terry.

"I don't know," said Steve. "I think we should include handlers. Only it should be tutus for the guys and ruffs for the girls."

"I ain't wearing a tutu," Jose said.

"But you'd look adorable," Bailey said, batting her eyes and waving an elegant hand.

"Can I wear my gun?" Terry asked.

"No," the others chorused.

"On that note, I'm heading into the park," Lia said.

Honey chased Kita across the park while Chewy began his usual patrol of the perimeter, this time from the inside. Lia and Bailey sat atop their favorite picnic table, under a hackberry tree.

"I still don't understand why you're using Chewy in the parade instead of Honey. Honey could do this blind-folded," Bailey said.

Lia sighed. "I was too busy for advanced classes when I got him. He needs the work."

"So you don't think his behavior has anything to do with him being a furry flibbertigibbet?"

"What on Earth is that?"

"I think it came from some Disney movie. It means he's flighty."

"Ouch."

"He's a funny little guy, but you have to admit, he's no Einstein. Not in the obedience arena."

Lia sighed. "Rub it in. He's ADHD. I'll need to carry liver treats to keep him focused."

"Perfectly legitimate. If they do it at dog shows, you can do it in the parade. Though, in his case, you may want to go for a pocket full of bacon."

Chewy trotted over and jumped up, bracing his forepaws on the table bench. He grinned. His beard was clotted with mud.

"Chewy! Ugh! You've been eating dirt again." Lia jumped off the table and led him over to the pump. "Come along, Mister Muddy Mouth. You aren't dragging dirt into the house."

Chewy lapped out of a bucket sitting under the pump, rinsing his beard clean in the process. He followed Lia back to the table while she muttered.

"How long has he been doing that?" Bailey asked.

"I don't know. He does it every so often, always has. I haven't given it much thought. Do you think it's a problem?"

"I was just reading about this." A line formed between Bailey's eyes as she searched her memory. "It could be caused by thyroid problems or issues with his pancreas, or even brain lesions. His diet may be insufficient, or he could just be bored. Chewing releases dopamine in dogs. You should rule out any medical problems."

"I had no idea. So eating dirt isn't an issue by itself? It won't hurt him?"

"Depends on where the dirt comes from. If it's loaded with pesticides, it'll be toxic. That's not an issue in the park, but dirt can wear his teeth down, and he can crack them on stones. He could wind up with an obstruction. If it's not medical, it would be a good idea to occupy him with a substitute."

Lia sighed. "I'm betting it's a habit left over from before. When I found him, he'd been neglected. Not abused, but it was obvious that someone dumped him in the back yard and ignored him. I don't think he'd ever been groomed. His coat was matted thicker than carpet. And he had so much eye-gunk matted in his fur, I don't know how he could see. Still, we'd better check it out." She leaned down, looked Chewy in the eyes and ruffled his ears. "You, Mister Muddy Mouth, are going to the vet."

Penny, Steve's small terrier mix, leapt up on the picnic table and lavished her usual frantic kisses on Lia's cheek before jumping down to make a play bow for Chewy, who grumbled and barked. Penny, undeterred, raced around the table in circles. As Penny usually played advance guard for Terry and Steve, Lia looked up to see them approaching, followed by Jackson and Napa.

Terry always reminded Lia of a stockier Teddy Roosevelt. Now that he and Steve were roommates, the pair often came to the dog park together. The two were of a size, though Steve was round and bald where Terry was chunky and hirsute. They reminded her of Tweedle-Dee and Tweedle-Dum.

No one understood how they managed to live together. Terry, a retired government worker, held rabidly right-wing views. Steve was a die-hard Democrat and former union negotiator who now worked at the Homeless Association. Steve once explained to Lia that they had a compromise Terry would not listen to Rush Limbaugh while Steve was home, and Steve would not turn on Bill Mahler while Terry was there. Together, they watched sports.

"What's the word, what's the word?" Terry asked.

"Flibbertigibit," Bailey volunteered.

"Ah, Wayland's exasperating apprentice," Terry said.

"Who?" Bailey asked.

"Wayland's Smithy is a neolithic barrow in England. Wayland was a god, and when his apprentice annoyed him too much, he threw the apprentice as far as he could. The boy turned into stone when he landed. He is now a boundary marker for Sniveling Corner."

Steve stared at Terry. "I'm going to block the History Channel."

"Too late," Lia said.

"What's going on with your friend Leroy?" Steve asked.

"He's not my friend," Lia said. "I've never met him."

"He's paying you to build a float. Doesn't that make him your friend?" Steve asked.

"You explain it," Lia told Bailey.

"Lia's not important enough to meet the author. She's been fobbed off on underlings," Bailey explained.

"His aunt and her friends manage the business for him," Lia said. "I guess he doesn't care about that end of things."

"Especially not since he's still missing," Bailey added. "I haven't seen anything new lately. But what's with that blogger? Is she really his girlfriend?"

"What blogger?" Lia asked.

"She calls herself 'Citrine.' I'm guessing that's because Pink is already taken. She's a singer-slash-poet-slash-blogger and wannabe internet personality. She has orange hair and angst."

"I don't get the orange hair and angst connection," Steve said.

"Orange is associated with happiness," Lia said. "That and highway barrels. Doesn't say 'angst' to me."

"You have a point," Steve said, "I've had plenty of angst over highway barrels."

"Black has been done to death." Bailey pulled up the internet on her phone. "Huh. This page says orange is also associated with 'emotional resilience during difficult times.' Maybe that's what she means."

"I thought citrine was yellow," Steve said.

"That's the color," Bailey said. "Citrine is also a type of quartz crystal, and it's orange."

"Look up the stone," Lia said.

Bailey tapped her screen again. "Oh. It's called the merchant's stone. Maybe she's hoping to make money off her internet stuff."

"So," Terry said. "is the mercenary wench attempting to profit from Leroy's current predicament?"

"Predicament meaning he might be dead? I hope not," Lia said.

"It's a weird fit. Lucas Cross fans are not her audience, though he is semi-famous. Anyone searching for him on the internet will come up with her page," Bailey explained. "And every hit counts. Even the extraneous hits will help her visibility."

"Maybe she's just a drama queen and she really loves him," Lia said.

Steve and Terry looked at each other. They shook their heads and said, "Nah," simultaneously.

"How's her poetry?" Steve asked.

"Uninspiring, with erotic intentions, except when she's wailing about Leroy's disappearance. She seems to like the idea that he's dead," Bailey said.

"Probably because a corpse can't tell everyone that she made it all up," Terry said.

"Does this person have a dog?" Steve asked.

"Cat, why?"

"Thank God," Lia said. "We won't run into her here."

Lia scraped the last bit of black paint out of the cup she held and was dabbing it on top of a gun sight the size of a flat-screen TV when the sound of a door closing echoed through the vast commercial garage. Lia looked down from her perch on a towering safety ladder to see Sarah Schellenger examining the float.

Sarah, librarian at the Northside branch library, was tall and slender with hair to the middle of her back and a forthright nose to go with her forthright sensibilities. She ran a knitting group at the library, informally named Fiber and Snark, where she created sweaters for teddy bears that she sold to raise money for SCOOP, an organization that aided management of the local feral cat population and provided medical care for feral cats with special needs. She and her husband, Duane, had eleven cats of their own.

Lia put her brush in the empty cup, then tucked both into a large pocket on her painting vest. "I think that's it for today," she yelled down.

"I don't know why you're bothering with the top," Sarah yelled back. "Who's going to see up there? Superman?"

"You never know when the Google Earth satellite will pass over."

"True."

Lia climbed down the monster ladder, though climbing didn't seem like the right word. The thing had 24 inch wide steps and handrails, for heavens sake, making it suitable for debutantes in hoop skirts.

She opened a dented and rusted folding chair and plopped down next to Sarah, sighing and rolling her head around to stretch her neck. Chewy scratched an ear and yawned from his nest of tarps by the wall. He rose from his nap and came over to demand an ear ruffle. Lia automatically obliged as she looked up at the gun, satisfied with their progress.

"Terry keeps saying the Browning Buckmark is only a .22 and unworthy of such exaltation, but I don't think anyone else cares," Lia said.

"Next time I need a 16 foot tall model of a gun, he can build it instead of just letting you take pictures of one," Sarah said. "The 24 inch PVC sewer pipe was the only thing light enough to work, and it was scrap, so I got it free. You found a gun with the right proportions and a round barrel. Tell him to pull on his big girl panties and suck it up."

The parade float dedicated to Lucas Cross' international crime thrillers was a marvel of engineering, built on the back of a flatbed trailer to a scale of 1:30. Lia had tapped Jose to help build the framework after Jim, a retired engineer, advised her on the plans.

The Browning Buckmark lacked the firepower of a .44 magnum, but its molded rubber grips swooped in lines that appealed to Lia's artist sensibilities. The black grips contrasted with the silver barrel and the gold trigger was a detail she couldn't resist. Everyone agreed that it screamed "international espionage."

The float would be finished with banners hanging from the sides of the trailer that advertised the upcoming twin launch of Lucas Cross' latest books, *Savage Gun* and *Koi: Predator.*

"Still no word about Leroy?" Lia asked.

Sarah sighed and looked down at the floor. "He's still missing. The Austin police won't tell us anything."

"Debby must be going crazy. I can't believe you're going ahead with the parade float."

"Alice made the point that if Lucas is still missing by July 4th, it will only be in slightly worse taste than the usual Northside parade float. The books are coming out next month, regardless."

Sarah looked at her watch. "I've got to help Cecilie feed the cats at SCOOP. Carol usually comes on Saturdays, but she's out of commission. Can I bribe you into giving me a hand?"

"Sure, I'll give you a hand, if you don't mind Chewy coming along."

Chewy lifted his head off his canvas bed and gave Sarah a grin.

Sarah looked at the schnauzer, evaluating. "I'm not worried. They've got him outsized and outnumbered."

SCOOP, which stood for Save Cats & Obliterate Over-Population, was Cecilie's feral cat sanctuary. It currently housed 88 cats. Lia was surprised when Sarah pulled up to a neatly landscaped brick house. Only Chewy's vigorous sniffing suggested anything was out of the ordinary.

"Looks too normal, doesn't it?" Sarah asked.

"Ninety cats? Here?" Lia asked.

"Eighty-eight at last count. We go through one thousand pounds of kitty litter every month."

Lia did the math. Cecile must go through a 35 pound bag of kitty litter every day. She was tossing out over 200 pounds of just kitty litter a week. *The garbage men must hate her.*

"Where do they come from?"

"There are dozens of feral cat colonies around Cincinnati. We assist in spay/neuter programs that release the cats back into the wild, but our primary goal is to home adoptable cats and provide sanctuary for those that have medical conditions that require ongoing treatment. Some have feline AIDS, some have leukemia. Others have been horribly abused. We take in litters when we can, to socialize the kittens for adoption. Cecilie is overloaded right now because someone was shooting the cats in a feral colony behind a trailer park. We had to get them out of there."

"You have cages for them all?"

"Most of them have the run of the first floor." Sarah opened her door. "Come on. I'll give you the tour."

Lia's progress up the front walk was hampered by Chewy's frantic sniffing. Finally Lia took a treat from her pocket and held it up for him. Cats forgotten, Chewy followed the lure to the house. Cecilie met them on the steps. Her wiry hair was shot with gray and scraped back into a practical bun. The crystal drops she wore on her ears made a feminine counterpoint to her striped tee and work jeans.

"Reinforcements! Excellent," Cecilie said. "The first thing we're going to do is clean the litter pans. Then we'll feed them. I'll take care of the quarantined cats after you leave."

"You have cats in quarantine?"

"Every cat goes through quarantine when it arrives to ensure it doesn't pass any diseases to the population. We also keep a few who are communicable. You won't be handling them."

"Cecilie wouldn't let the Centers for Disease Control touch those cats with hazmat suits and a ten-foot pole. She has high standards," Sarah said.

Chewy strained towards the door.

"Are you sure Chewy isn't going to be a problem?" Lia asked.

"If he is, they'll soon put him in his place," Cecilie said. "Just keep him on his leash until he calms down. I bet he finds a nice, safe corner for himself."

Cecilie led them into a small foyer with a 40-inch tall pet gate at the far end.

"I've got goodies for the closet," Sarah said, removing several leashes and a dog coat from her tote bag.

"Great." Cecilie turned to Lia. "We get a lot of donations. We raise money with garage sales, but we keep any dog and cat equipment that we can't use to pass along to other rescue organizations. Those donations have their own space."

Sarah opened the closet door. It was filled with every kind of leash and harness imaginable, along with a hodgepodge of grooming tools, food dishes, and collapsible crates. She hung the leashes on a hook, then placed the dog coat on a shelf with several others.

A marmalade cat strolled to the gate, rubbing itself against the vertical bars. Chewy lunged for the gate, barking. The cat looked up, as if to say, "What are *you* doing here?" then sat down and started cleaning itself. Chewy whined.

"I bet that cat knows exactly how far Chewy's paws would reach through those bars," Lia said.

"That's Jam, and you wouldn't be wrong," Sarah said.

Cecilie opened the gate and Jam leapt into a cat tree. The foyer opened up into a feline jungle. Cats perched on a half-dozen multi-level cat trees anchored to the ceiling to ensure feline acrobatics would not cause disaster. Cats strolled along the carpet-covered catwalks that lined every wall, seven feet above the floor.

Chewy whined and returned to Lia's side.

"Stranger in a strange land, Little Man?" Lia asked.

"We tried the cat walks at 6 feet," Cecilie said, "but the cats liked to lurk up there and swat at people passing by, so we raised them."

The living room furniture was covered with sheets tied around the legs, then topped with industrial pet covers that look like quilted mover's blankets. There was a four-foot path behind one sofa, where large litter boxes sat on larger quilted pads. Cardboard cat scratchers were strategically placed around the room. On one side, two four-foot wire cubes held a half-dozen cats each. The crates were topped with fleece canopies, serving double duty as cat hammocks.

The living room flowed into the dining room, which opened to the kitchen on one side and an enormous den on the other. The kitchen and den had pet gates.

Cecilie led Lia and Chewy into the den, where patio doors looked onto the back yard, which featured several bird feeders on poles and a pair of bird baths. More than a dozen cats sat, riveted, watching the birds.

"It's cat heaven," Lia said. "I can't believe how clean everything is. And you live here. Amazing."

"We love it," Cecilie said. She returned to the gate and pointed at a loose mounting. "Be careful when you use this gate. We need to fix it. Bill hasn't gotten around to it yet. It's one of a hundred things we haven't found time to do."

"Realities of a non-profit," Sarah said.

"Truth," Cecilie said.

Lia was scooping the last of a bag of kibble into a communal feed bowl when the front door opened.

Someone called out, "I'm here, let's get this show on the road. Where is everybody?"

"Damn," Sarah said, setting down a water dish.

"Who's that?" Lia asked.

"I have a confession to make."

"Let me guess. That's Paris Hilton. She's sponsoring all the cats and their personal attendants are on their way with coolers full of fresh tuna steaks."

"Not quite." Sarah sobered. "The members of Fiber and Snark want to talk to you. That's Debby. Alice and Carol will be here any minute."

They hate the float. Worse, they can't pay me for the float. A month away from my own work for nothing…

"Come on," Sarah said to Lia, "I'll finish this later."

Lia sat on a couch between Sarah and Cecilie as a parade of felines waltzed across the back and climbed down to knead laps with sharp claws. Chewy took refuge behind Lia's legs, whining in distress as a one-eyed Siamese rubbed against Lia's shin. She reached down to scratch his head, idly noticing the absence of cat hair on the furniture. *How many hours does Cecilie spend brushing them every day?*

Debby sat on another couch across the room. She was a sturdy, middle-aged woman with an abundance of thick, black hair that was her best feature. Lia bet she kept it long for simplicity rather than vanity. Her clothes were functional knits that likely came from a big box store. She looked like she had the temperament of a steamroller. She probably needed it. The Elmwood Place branch was one of the more difficult posts for a librarian.

Sarah and Debby gave each other odd looks and said nothing. Sarah looked down at the Persian in her lap while scratching her own scalp.

"You'd better not have fleas," Debby said.

"It's stress-induced dandruff."

"I hope it's not catching," Debby muttered.

The silence resumed until Lia heard a car pull up outside. Sarah's shoulders slumped in relief.

"It's about time," Debby said.

Alice opened the door. She was a freckled brunette with short, wavy hair and studious spectacles. She was an architect who specialized in rehabbing Northside Victorians and wore functional tunics in exotic prints that impressed clients with her creative sensibilities.

"Where's Carol?" Sarah asked.

"She's stumping along," Alice said, holding the door open as Carol, right leg encased in a clunky apparatus that looked like a toe-less ski boot, struggled through the door on a pair of crutches. The scrape on her forehead was now scabbed. Debby moved over to make room for her. Carol dropped down and sighed, a pair of tabbies dashing for cover as she let the crutches fall.

"A fracture boot? Isn't that overkill?" Debby asked.

"It's a very serious sprain," Carol sniffed.

"Will someone finally let me know what's going on?" Lia asked.

"We need your help," Sarah said.

Ruh roh. This sounds worse than getting stiffed for a 16-foot gun.

"We'd better start at the beginning," Alice said. "You know how we talked to you about doing covers for Leroy's books?"

"Yes," Lia said carefully.

"Hold on," Cecilie said. "Did she promise?"

"I haven't promised anything. What am I supposed to promise?" Lia asked.

"You can't tell anyone," Cecilie said.

Lia felt herself slipping down a rabbit hole. *What are they talking about? Tell them what?*

"You can't repeat anything we say here," Alice explained.

"And that includes your boyfriend, the detective," Cecilie said.

"Wait a minute," Lia said, holding up both hands, palms outward. "Is this something that would concern the police? I don't like keeping secrets from Peter."

"Technically, it's out of this jurisdiction. It wouldn't be his case," Alice said.

Lia frowned.

"Nobody knows a crime has been committed except us, and that may be a moot point," Carol said.

Sarah shook her head, sighing. "Look, can you just promise? Otherwise, we'll never get anywhere. We haven't committed a crime."

"You might get a different story if you talk to some of Leroy's reviewers on Amazon," Debby said. "Look, we know something that we probably should share with the authorities in a jurisdiction far, far away. But if we do that, we're going to be in worse trouble than being arrested."

"It'll cost millions," Carol moaned.

"Hush, Carol. She hasn't promised yet," Cecilie said.

Lia stood up. Two cats took her place on the sofa. She pulled Chewy's leash out of her pocket. "I think this is my cue to leave."

"Please don't go," Sarah said. "Will you hear us out?"

"What don't the Austin police know about Leroy's disappearance?" Lia asked. Chewy danced at her feet, ready to go.

"I told you she was sharp," Sarah said. "Will you promise?"

Lia sighed. "Am I going to regret this?"

"Probably. But please do it anyway. You're the only one we can trust to help us."

Lia worked the leash in her hands as she looked longingly at the door. Friendship came with responsibility. Besides, she'd come with Sarah. If she left, she and Chewy would have to walk home. The others could jump in any of three cars and mow her down before she got to the end of the block. That's if she could get out the door ahead of them. She could wind up at the bottom of a scrimmage before she got to the foyer. Then she'd be in worse condition than Carol. Chewy would escape and wind up in an animal testing lab.

She pushed the cats aside and sat down. They dropped in front of Chewy, hissing. He whined and curled behind Lia's legs. "I promise. On the condition that I won't become party to a crime."

"I can live with that," Cecilie said.

"I repeat: what are you keeping from the Austin police?"

The five women looked at each other, trying to decide what to say next. Lia waited, watching the mesmerizing flow of cats in the middle of the room. One-eyed Pete leapt off a cat tree and sent the rest scattering like fish in a pond.

Cecilie broke the silence. "We know where he went."

Lia was astounded. "You let the police send out national alerts, spend thousands looking for him, and you knew where he was the whole time?" Lia exploded. She glared at Debby. "You cried in front of God and network news cameras?" She pinned the women with her eyes. "You manipulated millions of people? For *what*?" She popped up again, followed by Chewy.

"It wasn't like that," Alice said quietly. "We just found out. Can we start over?"

"How far back are we going to go?" Sarah asked.

"It was fun in the beginning," Cecilie said. She took a brush out of a pocket on the arm of the sofa and began grooming a marmalade tom.

"What was fun?" Lia asked, taking her seat again. Chewy sighed and lay back down.

"We've had the knitting club at the Northside Library ever since Sarah was appointed Head Librarian," Cecilie said. "It's mostly gossip. We're the only ones who show up, except for the odd drop-in. Alice tells the most outrageous stories about her family and neighbors ... ." She noticed Alice giving her the evil eye. "You do, too, and that's what started it all." She turned back to Lia. "It was the bunny slippers."

Bunny Slippers?

"Alice came in one day and told us about her daughter's rabbit, Bugs. He'd been eyeing Alice's bunny slippers with what she later realized was lascivious intent—"

"You have to understand," Alice said. "These are not cute, fluffy bunny slippers. These are Monty Python killer rabbit slippers with gaping jaws in all their fanged glory."

"—So Alice was minding her own business, petting the cat. Suddenly Bugs jumps on one of her slippers. Remember, she was wearing them at the time. Bugs begins humping," Cecilie said.

"Oh, no," Lia breathed.

"Do you know what bunny spunk looks like?" Cecilie asked.

Lia shook her head, aghast.

"Alice does. Those slippers went right into the washer. When they came out, they went right back in. The next time Bugs sidled up to the bunny slippers with a come hither twitch of his nose, she tore them off and chased him down, waving the slippers and making so much racket, he never came near them again. We were laughing so hard we couldn't speak and finally Debby says, 'This is just like Mitford, but with hippies and drive-bys.'"

"Mitford?" Lia asked.

"A series of books about small town eccentrics. Alice started writing her stories down and bringing them to knitting club. We all chimed in with ideas. She couldn't publish them because she'd get run out of Northside. Debby suggested changing the names and publishing under a pseudonym as an ebook, just for fun."

"We didn't expect to make any money," Alice said. "But that was during the Indie boom, when the only books you could get for your Kindle were over-priced best sellers and 99 cent books by nobody you ever heard of."

"I hear 99 cent books made a number of writers wealthy," Lia said.

"We weren't Amanda Hocking, but we were making hundreds of dollars every month. We put it all into SCOOP," Alice said. "Then Carol read Russell Blake's interview in the *Wall Street Journal*, and everything changed."

Lia gave her a puzzled look.

"Russell Blake made two million dollars with his ebooks in less than three years," Carol explained. "He was very open about how he made that money, which was through a grueling schedule of writing and publishing eight to ten books a year."

Lia's eyes went round at the thought of that much work.

"I looked into it," Carol continued. "Most writers making big money publish at least six times a year. I said it was superhuman for one person to write eight books a year, but five people could put out ten books a year."

"It was a joke," Sarah said. "We decided that to make that much money, we couldn't collaborate on funky books about neighborhood weirdos, we'd have to write in one of the high dollar genres. That meant either romance or thrillers."

"We knew we couldn't stomach writing romance," Alice said, shuddering, "even though the market for romance is voracious, and twice as big as the next largest market. Crime fiction was next in line."

"We pretended to be Russell Blake wannabes," Sarah said. "We invented a hot, female super-spy named Koi and patterned her after Russell Blake's *Jet* series, but with significant differences. We made up outrageous stories, take-offs on all the best sellers."

"All while you were knitting?" Lia asked, fascinated. She scratched the head of one of the deposed tabbies, who'd decided to share Lia's seat with her.

"It was easy. We're all readers, and we have two librarians. We know our stuff," Cecilie said. "We decided to make up a pen name based on popular protagonists in that market, and came up with—"

"Lucas Cross," Lia said.

"Then *one* day, *Sarah* says, 'you know, we could do this, only we need a guy who will let us use his photo for the author page. Nobody will think anything of it not being his real name. Russell Blake isn't a real name. '"

Lia stated the obvious. "They aren't Leroy's books."

"We needed a macho man to sell the series. No one would buy thrillers written by a group of middle-aged knitters. Leroy is the face of our brand," Alice said.

Lia took a moment to process this. "He has nothing to do with the books?"

"He didn't even know about them until Lucas Cross was invited to do a signing at Joseph Beth. Leroy hasn't opened a novel since they taught *To Kill a Mockingbird* in tenth grade, and I doubt he ever read more than two pages of it. But we needed a good-looking guy who knew how to BS. He fit the bill, and paying him a percentage got him out of my sister Dorothy's house. Saved her marriage, too, though that's taken a big hit since Leroy vanished." Debby said.

"If he doesn't read books, how did he pull off signings?" Lia asked, fascinated.

Carol yelped as a cat clawed at her boot, using it for a scratching post. Debby pushed it away.

"He'd tell them he just got back from some exotic place and make up a story about the bars and a street brawl, then he'd read a page out of the book, Debby said. "He comes by his ability to lie naturally. We had to coach him on reading out loud. He knows how to charm women, and anytime anyone asked him anything touchy, he just told them he was under a non-disclosure agreement and changed the subject. We're self-published. I don't know why none of those dumb bunnies ever asked him how you can be under a non-disclosure agreement with yourself."

"Well, that's neither here nor there," Sarah said. "It worked fine until George Weir invited Leroy to be on a panel discussion at AustinCon.

"Who?" Lia asked.

"Doesn't matter. What does matter is that *some of us*"— Debby glared at Alice and Sarah—"Felt it was *im-*

portant to accept. *Some of us* wouldn't listen to those of us who knew Leroy all his life, and *some of us* thought they could tutor him, and he'd be able to pull it off."

"What really happened in Austin?" Lia asked, suddenly realizing the women had lulled her into a dangerous complacency.

"Alice, you do the honors. I'm still too upset to talk about it," Debby said.

"Have you been following the papers?" Alice asked.

"I've picked up headlines on the internet." Lia said.

"A quick recap: Leroy disappeared during Austin-Con, and it looked like he snuck down to the basement to meet with someone. There was evidence of a fight. There was no sign of him after that. We think he was smuggled out in a blue van, but there was no proof."

"All that was in the news," Lia said.

"That was a week ago," Alice continued.

"An endless, miserable week being questioned by the police, hiding from reporters and listening to Dorothy blame me at the top of her lungs," Debby said.

"Three days ago, he called me," Alice said.

Lia blinked. "Why would he call you instead of his mother or Debby?" Lia asked.

"Probably because he knew there was no way we could have a rational conversation, with what he had to say," Debby said.

"It was a hoax," Sarah said. "He thought disappearing from AustinCon would give the new books a boost and get him off the hook for the panel."

"He acted like he did us a favor. He expected us to think he was smart," Alice said.

"Don't forget the part about laying on the beach in Belize." Cecilie said.

"He didn't think about how he was going to make his reappearance." Debby leaned forward. The cat in her lap yowled and jumped down. "Can you say 'fraud'? How about 'creating a panic'? I've never seen anyone put so much effort into doing something so stupid. He didn't put out that much effort in thirteen years of public education."

"So, he's in Belize?" Lia asked.

"We thought so, but we have reason to believe he's not there, if he ever was."

"And nobody knows outside this room?" Lia asked.

"Not even his mother," Debby said. "Better she continue to think he was kidnapped by pirates than he ran off on purpose without caring about her feelings."

"What did you tell him?" Lia asked.

"I didn't," Alice said. "I was asleep when he called. Good thing, too. I would have blown out all the cell towers between here and Central America giving him a piece of my mind."

"You mentioned money earlier," Lia said. "Where does that fit in?"

"Leroy's shenanigans are not only illegal, they could expose us and ruin our brand," Carol said. "And hiring an attorney to defend him could cost us everything we've made so far. If we're implicated in this mess, you can multiply the legal fees by six."

"Carol's our accountant, can you tell?" Cecilie said.

"You don't want to go to the police?" Lia asked.

"Not yet," Sarah said.

"What are they going to do, besides blow the whole thing wide open?" Carol asked. "Extradition with Belize is a murky area. They can't drag him home. *If* he's even there."

"But it's more serious than money now. Carol believes Leroy attacked her last night." Alice said.

"You never did like him," Debby accused.

Carol drew herself up. Lia swore she saw the top of her poof of red hair raise up like the hackles on a dog. "I only said he might not be reliable. He's not here now, which means I was right."

"Leroy was your mugger?" Lia asked.

"I caught a whiff of Dunhill cologne right before I fell. It's his favorite. It costs $250 a bottle. You won't find many muggers wearing it." Carol glared at Debby. She batted another cat away and slipped two fingers under her support boot, rubbing her leg in a way that suggested she wanted a vigorous scratch, but was too ladylike to do it in public.

"We don't know for sure that it was him, but we have to consider that possibility," Alice said.

"Maybe it was someone trying to make you think it was Leroy," Lia said.

"We thought of that," Alice said. "But who would spend that much money on the off chance Carol would recognize the scent while he was mugging her?"

"Why would Leroy attack Carol?" Lia asked.

"I had a practice session with Leroy before we left for Austin," Carol said. "He kept arguing with the way we wanted him to approach the panel topic. It came out that he felt he deserved a bigger piece of the pie and creative input. Said it was his face, and if he represented the books, he ought to have a voice in them. I told him it would never happen."

"I wish you hadn't done that," Sarah said. "We could have listened to his ideas. It wouldn't have hurt anything. We listen to everyone's ideas. If they don't work, we don't use them."

"Like you don't use my ideas," Carol muttered.

"Water? Bridge?" Debby said.

"Why tell me? I don't see what I can do about your situation," Lia said.

Four pairs of eyes turned to look at Sarah. Lia followed their gaze.

"That was my idea," Sarah admitted. "When Alma told me about you, she also mentioned some of your, uh, adventures."

Lia groaned.

"She's very proud of you," Sarah said. "I had the sense from things she didn't say, that you have ... resources you might be able to tap in our cause. We need to know what happened to Leroy. We need to find him and figure out a way to resolve his disappearance without exposing Lucas Cross as a fraud."

"We need to know if he's behind Carol's attack," Alice said, "and if he meant to kill her."

"And I told you," Debby said, "stop drinking your own damn Kool-Aid. Leroy isn't smart enough to pull this off."

"It happened in Koi number seven, 'Death Happens Twice.' He did a lot of signings for that one. He had to pick up the plot, even if by osmosis," Alice said. "And who says he didn't have help. Maybe he's smart enough to find someone who could pull it together."

"But why? What reason would he have to kill Carol? That's what you all think, isn't it, that someone tried to kill Carol by shoving her down those stairs?" Lia asked.

"The way our bylaws read," Carol said, "if anything happens to one of our members, the partnership is dissolved and has to be reformed. That means everything is up for negotiation."

"But that's killing the goose that laid the golden egg!" Debby insisted. "Without all of us, there are no books."

"And how often does that happen in real life?" Cecilie pointed out. "Maybe he wants to create a vacancy in our little cabal. Maybe he sees himself stepping in. Maybe he told Alice he was in Belize to throw us off track."

"There's another thing," Debby said. "In every plot I ever read where someone is behind their own disappearance, they fall off a boat and are presumed dead so nobody will look for them. That's not what happened here."

Cecilie looked at Debby levelly. "You tell me with a straight face that boy has the enterprising spirit to swim a quarter mile to shore in the dark."

"You do have a point."

"He barely has the initiative to pull the tab on his beer," Cecilie elaborated.

"You don't have to grind it in," Debby said.

"What do you want me to do?" Lia asked.

"We may be off track," Alice said, "but Sarah thought you might have an *alternative* means to track Lucas. If you do, we're begging you to help us find him."

Damn Peter! He must have said something to Alma. That's the only way Sarah could know about Trees. Lia sighed.

47

The hacker would do anything for Bailey, but this was different. She thought about the month she'd spent building the float instead of working on her own paintings. Now these women wanted more from her. The internal struggle lasted for a few, tense seconds before falling to social pressure. *How much time can it take to ask Bailey to pass this along to Trees?*

"I can see if anything can be done, but it's not up to me. And it will cost. I have no idea how much."

"That's all we're asking," Alice said. She gave Carol a hard look. "I'm sure the price, whatever it is, will be worth it."

Lia pulled out her smart phone. "Let me record this. I promise I won't share it with anyone. It will save time later."

The group looked at each other, hesitated as if no one wanted to be responsible for saying yes or no to this.

Sarah stood up. "I need to get back to the cats."

"I do too," Cecilie said. A feline parade followed them out of the room.

"It's either that," Lia said to the remaining trio, "or writing everything down. I guarantee, that *someone*, like my boyfriend the detective, is more likely to run across notes on paper than an audio recording." Her point made, she opened the app and turned it on. "First things first. I'm going to need the numbers of his credit cards and bank accounts."

More grumbles.

"We start by following the money. It's possible to dig out that information without your help, but that wastes time. You want help, I need the info. I also need to know Leroy's friends, any girlfriends, anyone he would go to for help in an emergency, and how you think he would be getting around."

Carol produced a sheet of paper from her purse. "All of his accounts are listed here."

Lia looked at Alice. "I need the number he called you from, and copy of the message he left."

The number is in my call log, but I don't have the message anymore," Alice said. "I must have erased it by accident."

"Write down what you remember," Lia said. She turned to Debby. "Names, addresses, and phone numbers of his friends."

"Hold on, you're not going to talk to them, are you? You can't do that," Debby said.

"Not at all. But if he has an accomplice, it's likely to be one of them, don't you think?"

"If it is, they plotted it out while they were drunk. Then this would all make sense," Debby said.

"What about Citrine?" Lia asked.

"That tart claiming she's Leroy's own true love? The one who looks like the Little Match Girl caught her hair on fire and didn't know enough to put it out? She ought to call herself Cinder instead."

"Cinder for Cinderella?"

"Cinder for burnt to a crisp."

"You don't like her."

"Never heard of her until she showed up at the last press conference. Leroy never brought her around, and I've got news for her, Leroy doesn't have girlfriends. He has booty calls. As far as Leroy's concerned, this grand passion has all the heat of a dead LED."

"If you've never met her, how do you know this?" Lia asked.

"That's how I know it. He's a mama's boy. If he cared for her, he'd introduce her and show her off to the family."

Hands covered in flour, Peter Dourson shoved at the hair falling into his eyes with his elbow. When this failed, a jerk of his head shook the wayward strands back in place. He sunk his hands back into the bowl of gluten-free dough sitting on the kitchen counter in Lia's apartment.

Lia had an odd fanaticism about her diet, saying she could not afford to get sick. He'd never known her to get a cold, but he wasn't sure great health was worth the sacrifice of eating gluten-free pizza. *What a man won't for love. At least it's only for 90 days.*

Viola, his chow mix, perked her ears and launched herself across the floor in a thunder of scrabbling claws. Honey followed, both dogs barking excitedly. A key turned in the front door, followed by the expected tail thumps.

. Chewy announced himself with a yip.

"Honey, I'm home," he called.

Lia's laughter drifted down the hall. "Isn't that supposed to be my line?"

She grinned wickedly when she saw the gooey state of his hands.

"Looks like you're at my mercy," she said.

"Oh...help...please...don't—" he deadpanned his protests until Lia silenced him with a kiss.

"—Somebody save me."

"After dinner. I'm hungry. What are you making?"

"Spelt pizza. Gluten-free and totally on your bloody diet."

"That's Blood Type Diet, Kentucky Boy." She wrapped her arms around him from behind, avoiding the dough. "You're still my hero. What can I do to help?"

"It's under control," he said, nodding at the waiting array of chopped vegetables. "Feed the dogs?"

By now, all three dogs were swarming around them, bumping knees, wrangling for attention. Lia plowed through the roiling mass of fur to the kibble bin. She gave her dog pack a stern look.

"Down," she said.

The dogs lay on the floor, though Viola was sulky about it. They knew the drill.

"I thought you were going to be home sooner," Peter said as Lia shoveled kibble into the dog bowls. "Is everything okay with the float?"

Lia checked her conscience and decided it was clean. She kept her eyes on the bowls as she set them on the floor, then waved her hand to release the dogs.

"Sarah needed help feeding the cats at SCOOP. They have 88 cats now."

"How did that happen?"

"They rescued a cat colony that someone was using for target practice."

Peter took a moment to consider the logistics of wrangling 88 cats. "That must have been some trick. I imagine the local rednecks are pissed they've lost their entertainment."

"I'd like to shoot a few rounds at them and see how they like it," Lia said.

"Yes, but since you're civilized, you won't."

"Since they'd shoot back, I won't."

"Good girl."

Dogs now contentedly crunching their kibble, Lia headed for the refrigerator. "I'm getting some tea. Want some?"

"Is it real tea, or stuff that looks like death warmed over?"

"Stinging nettle lattes may not look like much but I feel so much better since I gave up coffee."

"That's not true. I can testify that you felt just as amazing when you were still mainlining caffeine."

Lia smacked him on the hip pocket of his Levi's. "Pervert."

"I'll be ready for a beer as soon as I get this dough rolled out." He pulled a firm ball of dough out of the bowl, kneaded it a handful of times on a patch of flour on the counter and set it on an oiled cookie sheet. He patted and prodded the dough until it was vaguely flat and oblong.

"Aren't you skipping a step?" Lia asked. She was sipping on her tea, which was an ugly greenish-gray that Peter had only ever seen in the morgue, and once in the sky before a tornado.

"If you loved me, you wouldn't drink that in a glass I can see through."

"If I loved you, I'd toss out your Pepsi and Pop Tarts. I can't believe my big, bad cop is so squeamish about the color green."

"Green is my favorite color," Peter said, reaching for the rolling pin and giving it a quick dusting of flour. "It's the color of your eyes. The slop you like to make is never green. It's always one of green's mutant cousins."

Lia looked down at her glass. "I can't argue that. By the way, Sarah says she saw you the other day."

"Oh?"

"She's buying the house next to Alma's. She and Alma were on the porch, waiting for the home inspector when you left for work. She thinks you're hot."

"She sounds like a woman with good taste."

"As long as she keeps her good taste to herself. I don't know if I want her living by you."

Peter grinned over his rolling pin. He kept his voice neutral as he rolled the dough out to the edges of the cookie sheet. "You don't have much time to do anything about it if she's already meeting with inspectors. She must be determined to have that house. There were a number of people who wanted it, even in the condition it's in."

"What's wrong with it? The house is beautiful."

"Sure, on the outside. Ruth Peltier was a hoarder. Alma did a reverse mortgage deal with her years ago to help her out. She made sure the exterior and the yard were kept up, but she could never convince Ruth to liquidate her belongings. You can't paint walls you can't reach. No one has seen the floors in decades.

Alma doesn't want to get into managing property, so she's selling the house 'as is,' with all the contents. I had my eye on it, until she told me how much work needed to be done. That was too much, on top of the bidding war."

"You want to buy a house?"

Peter shrugged and set the rolling pin aside. "The right house would be a solid investment. What I really want is a nice Craftsman, with a long porch and dormer windows. I was thinking about you, though."

"I like living in an apartment. No maintenance."

"If you bought it, I'd be two houses over and you'd have extra income renting out the other floor. But that one is too much work. Moot point, since it's now your friend's problem."

"That's so sweet."

Peter cocked a stern eyebrow when she reached for a diet-forbidden kalamata olive. She pouted, then satisfied herself with a strip of roasted red pepper. "I'd love having you for a neighbor, but I'm not ready for home ownership."

He shrugged again. "It was a thought."

"A very nice one. Maybe one day when I'm more settled, I'll have time for a house."

"It wouldn't be so tough if it were both of us. Together, we could do a house."

"Peter, I don't know …."

"I practically live here now."

"True. … but I like having my own place."

"We've been seeing each other long enough. Shouldn't we be thinking about the next level?"

"Is that what a house means to you? That I love you and want to stay with you?"

"Well, uh," *Where is she coming from?* "It's part of the package."

"What if I love you and want a future with you and have my own space?"

"Renting two so-so apartments for more money than we would spend buying a great house doesn't make any sense."

"It doesn't make sense financially. It makes sense relationally. Our relationship is more important to me than money."

"I'm glad to hear it, but I don't follow your logic."

"A friend of mine made her husband sell his giant bust of Sylvester Stallone as Rocky—complete with sweat dripping down his face— at a yard sale for $10 because she couldn't live with it. If they lived apart, he could have kept it, he could do his laundry when he damn well pleased and they would have eliminated half of the conflict in their relationship. As it is, if they ever get divorced, he's going to regret getting rid of Rocky for the rest of his life."

"I never liked Rocky anyway."

"You have your own Rocky. You have that monstrous TV taking up half of your living room with that hideous sofa taking up the other half so you can crash out and watch sports."

"We'd have a den for that."

"You don't need to stake out your personal territory if you have your own place. Your whole apartment is your personal territory. And when I'm there, I'm a guest, and if I don't like the way you do things, it doesn't matter because I have things my own way in my space."

"I don't want you to feel like a guest when we're together."

"Have you ever noticed that people who live together feel free to get angry at each other over stupid things? Guests are so much more civil. Living apart takes a lot of tension out of a relationship. Oprah and Stedman have been a couple for 30 years and never lived together."

Peter kept his voice carefully neutral. "You've given this a lot of thought."

"I have. I've thought about our future." She set her tea down and brushed the hair off his forehead. "For the first time in my life, I want to have a future with someone. I know what I'm like. I'm like a plant that needs a certain amount of shade to thrive. I'd rather spend four nights a week with you for the next 30 years than seven nights a week for the next three, which is how long I would last before I freaked and went bananas. And there you would be, missing your ugly sofa."

Peter shook his head. He didn't know what to say.

Lia took his face in her hands. "Do you love me and want to be with me, the way things are? Because I never want to be without you."

Peter held up a flour-covered hand with the little finger crooked. "Pinky swear?"

"With a kiss." She hooked her finger with his and stood on tip-toes with lips pursed.

Peter paused a breath away from her lips, until her eyes narrowed with annoyance. He tugged her closer with his pinky and brushed her mouth with his until her lips softened, then dived into the kiss. *Whatever this is, it's never boring.*

"Can we talk about dinner now?" Lia asked.

Peter, gratified by the flush rising in her face, used the back of his hand to brush a smudge of flour off her nose. "What about dinner?"

"Where's the pizza sauce?"

"No sauce. Olive oil. Alma contributed roasted garlic cloves, so I thought we'd do a slight variation on Dewey's Edgar Allen Poe."

"My hero. Can I help you decorate the pie?"

"You can do your half."

Lia laid toppings on her side of the pizza in a dizzying pattern that was heavy on garlic and artichoke with accents of sun-dried tomatoes and roasted red pepper slices. Peter shook his head when she dotted the top with pesto in a serpentine pattern.

"You know we're going to dump cheese all over everything, don't you?"

"It tastes better when it's pretty. Just ask the Japanese."

"Uh huh. It tastes better when it goes in my mouth."

"Philistine."

"I love it when you talk dirty."

Peter followed Lia's gaze down to three upturned, drooling, canine muzzles.

"Can we spread cheese out to the edges?" Lia asked. "I always feel so guilty when we give them crusts that have nothing on them. It doesn't seem fair."

Huh. How about you put your cheese on your half wherever you want and I'll do the same? The snarky thought vanished as soon as it appeared. Sometimes it was hard to remember Lia's phobia about conflict when she acted so logical. Her feelings ran so deep she had to protect herself or walk around like an open wound. He suspected her therapist and Bailey were the only other people who knew how vulnerable she was.

She did have a point. Signing a loan on a house was not proof of devotion. Hadn't his ex-fiancee Susan proven that? Lia was wrong about Rocky though. It wasn't the things he gave up for Susan that he had regretted, it was the home they never made.

"How about you do the honors?" The offer was a small, personal penance, but he got a kick out of Lia's judicious placement of cheese. While it covered to the edge, none of it extended beyond. When the pizza came out of the oven, there wasn't a shred of burned cheese on the cookie sheet. Lia said it was because the dogs stood guard over the oven, and it wouldn't dare fall off.

Pizza consumed, and cheesy crusts delivered to the dogs, Peter settled on the couch with a beer, leaning so that his head rested against the back. Lia curled next to him and ran her hand through his hair. "You got it cut. What's the occasion?"

They're going ahead with the restructuring. Our new captain came for a tour today. Captain Roller said he didn't want her to mistake me for a perp."

"Her?"

"Captain Ann Parker, from District Two. She's got quite the cop face. I have no idea what she thinks of her new command, but I swear I saw her eye twitch when she saw how small our interview room is."

"I imagine she'll get used to it. What happens when they centralize Major Crimes? Will you leave District Five?"

"They haven't announced who will go downtown. Heckle and Jeckle are chomping at the bit to go. I won't complain if they do."

"What about you? Don't you want to go?"

"There are as many reasons to stay as to go. I'm fine, either way."

"You don't want to be a top homicide cop?"

"I don't mind that part. I mind the part about working 30 hours straight every time I get a case and having to go all over the city, investigating people I don't know, working with cops I've never met before. I might never see you again."

"Peter, promise me you won't turn a promotion down because of me. I don't want to stand in the way of your career."

"Don't worry about it. They probably won't offer it to me."

Lia gave him a searching look. "By the way, the gang keeps asking me about Leroy Eberschlag."

"Them and everyone else. Austin isn't sharing. Brent was appointed local liaison, but I suspect that's going to be a one-way relationship."

"Brent? Why didn't they appoint someone with more seniority?"

"Roller doesn't confide in me, but I think it's a combination of two things. Brent's the only one I know who can look like he's kissing up without losing his manliness."

"And what's number two?"

"It's a nuisance detail. We aren't aware of any local connections to his disappearance, and Austin isn't putting any energy here. They haven't shared files with us. They want Brent to hold Dorothy Eberschlag's hand and not bug them while they do real cop work."

"What do you think happened?"

"Either Leroy took off on his own, or the kidnappers didn't know him well enough to know he doesn't write those books."

Lia bolted upright. "He doesn't?"

"I have no proof, just a hunch and circumstantial evidence."

"How do you figure it?"

"I ran him in a couple times for Drunk and Disorderly when I was a patrolman. When I heard he was a best-selling author and putting out six books a year, I couldn't believe it. I couldn't imagine him as a writer or having the work ethic to pull it off, so I did a little research. All the books are published and copyrighted by Bang Bang Books. I checked the filing of their LLC. Leroy isn't one of the partners. He's supposed to be one of the kings of self-publishing, but he has no control over the books."

"Oh."

"The partners are all middle-aged ladies. Two are librarians. I don't remember their names, but I suspect they're the women who hired you. I think he's just a front. The ladies might be willing to ransom him, but they don't really need him. He sure can't ransom himself. Anyone close to the situation would have picked up on the discrepancies."

"Have you told Austin any of this?"

"I figure they can do their own research. Anyway, I don't think the ladies would appreciate me letting the cat out of the bag. The Austin police can be the bad guys. I have to live here."

Chapter 3

Sunday, June 19

Thanks to recent hip surgery, John Morgan, whose hacker handle was "Trees," sat in his treehouse. He hadn't climbed the ancient white oak for more than 20 years due to progressive deterioration of his spine and hips that left him disabled. The climbing harness pinched his new hips painfully on the trip up, but it didn't diminish his exhilaration. *I'll make a sling to sit in for the next run, like window washers use. That should take care of it.*

He unclipped his harness and ascenders, unslung his knapsack, then leaned against the trunk of the elm, his heart still pounding. He wheezed heavily, his breath loud against the backdrop of wind shushing through the leaves and the twittering of birds. Sweat ran into his hair—streaked with gray and grown past his shoulders—and a beard that reached the middle of his chest because he'd been too fatigued to cut it during his convalescence.

He'd pay for over-exerting himself, but the trip had been worth it. His sky house had taunted him for too long, 30 feet from his front porch and impossible to reach.

Sunlight dappled two decades of dead leaves littering the weathered, gray floor of his aerie, a sturdy platform eight feet square and 40 feet in the air. His heart rate slowed, his breath evened out, and the pain in his hips faded.

He stayed where he was for several more minutes with his eyes closed, enjoying the breeze, the dancing bits of sunlight on his face, and the surrounding green. Even with his eyes closed, he could feel the life around him, taste the oxygen rich air. A tear snuck out from under one eyelid. This was home.

By some miracle, the old broom was still there, lodged between the platform and a pair of overhanging branches. The paint on the handle was peeling and the straw was filthy and fragile, but he was able to shove the accumulated leaves and debris over the side with it.

His knapsack yielded a yoga mat, a zabuton meditation mat and a zafu cushion. Cuddled in the zabuton was a Buddha statuette, twin of the one on his shrine in the living room. Buddha liked high places, and this treehouse was the highest place for miles around. He lodged the statuette in the crook of two branches, then used bungie cords to strap him in so he would survive high winds. He attached an empty Gatorade bottle below, as a repository for petitions. He draped a string of tiny magnasite skull carvings around the whole to enhance intuition and spiritual connection. Lastly, the knapsack coughed up a jade figure of a seated monkey, his personal animal totem.

The monkey was last year's Christmas gift from Bailey. He grinned, anticipating her next visit. Bailey had generous hands, graceful as swans, and they soothed his damaged body and wounded soul with delicate touches like the wings of birds.

He wondered if he could keep his new flexibility secret from her until November. That's when she closed her gardening business for the winter. It would be fun to surprise her.

He'd been mum earlier, when she called about the missing author. Leroy Eberschlag's digital footprint ended at the Austin Hyatt, if you didn't count the one phone call. That call came from a pre-paid cell phone currently pinging in Cincinnati. He followed the trail of pings back to Austin, where the phone had been activated the day after Leroy vanished.

According to the phone, Leroy arrived in Cincinnati several days later. How was the man living? He couldn't go out in public. Research into his friends uncovered no unusual activity that would suggest they were helping him. It was time for alternative methods.

This would be an appropriate christening of his treetop shrine. He placed a slip of paper into the Gatorade bottle, a request for the truth about Leroy's whereabouts. He lowered himself upon the zafu in a semi-kneeling position, with his knees on the zabuton underneath. The lotus position was beyond him, but this he could do.

John began his meditation with a simple prayer for clear vision, then emptied his mind, focusing instead on sensation. The clean sweat on his brow dried and cooled. A weight grew on one ankle. Metal walls enclosed him, cocoon-like. He heard a low hum and tasted stale air conditioning. His heart grew buoyant, filling the stale box. The box sat in a wasteland that stretched as far as the eye could see. A beautiful woman with gun-metal grey eyes watched.

John opened his eyes, disappointed. This was one of his more surreal visions. It happened sometimes. His visions always made sense, but there were times when understanding came only in retrospect. He reminded himself that Spirit always sent what he needed and the fault was with him for not interpreting correctly.

Wherever Leroy was, there was a sense of confinement and isolation, yet the heart was purposeful and at peace. Not a state of mind he would associate with being a victim or a mugger. And the woman, who was she?

Chapter 4

Monday, June 20

"The phone records say he's here, but Buddha and the jade monkey say he's in an air conditioned box in the middle of a wasteland and he's happy?" Lia turned to look at Bailey, amazed.

The two women sat on their favorite picnic table, enjoying the cool hours after sunrise before the humidity set in. For now they had the park to themselves. Honey nosed Lia's hand. She glanced down at the tennis ball she forgot she'd been holding. She lobbed it into the air so it would roll down the hill. Honey loped away, Chewy on her tail.

"Are you sure Trees isn't a lunatic?" Lia asked. "How can Leroy be here and somewhere else? What wasteland? How would he get there? And why? The conference is over. Why wouldn't he just come home?"

"Trees doesn't know if his vision was meant to be taken literally or not. There's plenty of wasteland out west. He could be in the western panhandle. It could be Death Valley. The border to Mexico is hours from Austin. There are places where people cross, if you know where they are. It wouldn't be hard to fly under the radar, especially if he had money."

"But Leroy didn't have any cash, not that anyone knows about. The ladies kept him on a tight leash so he wouldn't run off to Vegas and go on a bender. This is impossible."

"I wondered about it, too. I did a Tarot card reading about it." Bailey pulled a slim stack of the oversized cards out of her pocket.

Lia kept her face carefully neutral. She loved Bailey, but didn't buy into her New Age mumbo-jumbo. Friendship required that she listen, and be polite.

"The first card, the one representing the foundation of the situation was The Moon." Bailey laid a card on the picnic table, between them. In it, two funny-looking dogs howled at the night sky. "This represents deception, illusion, confusion, and things unknown. It means more is going on than we understand."

Well, duh.

"The second card describes the present." The card she turned over featured a man hanging upside-down from a wood post by one foot, the other leg cocked at the knee. His hands were behind his back, as if bound. She placed it to the left of the first card, at an angle.

"He certainly looks confined to me." *Better to humor her.*

"This card isn't about confinement. It means being powerless, needing to surrender to circumstances. Sometimes it's about sacrifice. It could also mean he's taking time out to gain a new perspective."

"Do you think he's been kidnapped?"

"It could just as easily mean he decided to take off and sort his head out."

"In the middle of a convention where crowds of adoring fans were waiting to fawn all over him? What kind of spiritual crisis would drive him to leave?"

"I haven't got it figured out, but the important thing to keep in mind when you draw cards is not only the cards you pull, but the ones that don't show up."

"Like what?"

"The Devil, which would mean he caved to temptation or addiction or malice; the seven of swords, which says he's pulling a fast one; ten of swords has all the swords stuck in a body. ..."

"I see your point. What's next?"

Bailey placed the third card directly above the first. "This is the advice card." On it, a young man held up a sword. "It means to seek the truth."

Lia didn't bother to roll her eyes. One card remained in Bailey's hand.

"So what's the last one?"

"It's the probable outcome. I don't like it." The card Bailey placed on the right featured a tower struck by lightning and two people falling out.

"I can see why. Good thing we don't have any towers around here."

"It can refer to any kind of catastrophe, or just a sudden event that destroys your foundations. It goes back to the Moon." Bailey pointed a graceful finger at the first card. "The first card says we don't know what's really going on. The last says the truth will come out, it will change everything, and it won't be gentle."

Lia tried to be diplomatic. "That's good, Bailey, but how does it help us? It doesn't tell us anything we don't already know."

Bailey pulled a card out of her other pocket. "I pulled one extra card, for our next step.

The card featured three women dancing and toasting each other with goblets.

"What does that mean?"

"The two main meanings are celebration and sisterhood."

"So we're supposed to party?"

"I'm still meditating on this one. I think we need to keep our eyes open. Something is hinky."

"What's kinky?" Steve asked as he and Terry approached their table. Steve's dog, Penny, jumped up on the picnic table and slashed her exuberant tongue across Lia's face. Lia urged her down.

"Enough, Penny." She gave Bailey a look. She wasn't sure what to tell Steve and Terry, if anything. Bailey shrugged.

"Your brain," Lia and Bailey said, simultaneously.

Steve roared.

"What's the news on Eberschlag, Lia?" he asked. "You're in a prime position to pick up gossip while you work on the float."

"There's nothing. Nobody knows what to think."

"I say it's a publicity stunt. I imagine all the press hasn't hurt his sales any. He's got a book coming out soon." Terry took out his phone and hunted up the Lucas Cross Amazon page on the browser. "*Savage Gun* ranks in the top 100 Kindle books. That's pre-orders."

"If he's dead, he's not going to care how many books he sells," Steve said. "Didn't they find blood at the scene?"

"Traces smeared on the wall, like someone wiped it up in a hurry," Lia said. "It tested positive for human blood. It will take weeks for the DNA to come back, if they had enough to test."

"Can't Peter find out about that?" Bailey asked.

"He says the Austin police are being closed-mouth. Brent told him being their Cincinnati liaison is like being told to go sit in the corner. So far they haven't asked him to do anything."

"No ransom demand?" Steve asked.

"Not that anyone knows of," Lia said. "It's possible Leroy's parents are in contact with kidnappers and aren't telling the police."

"Has Leroy made enough on his books to attract kidnappers?" Bailey asked.

Lia shrugged. "There were bigger names at the conference. Why go after Leroy when they had two New York Times best selling authors on the panel he missed?"

"He was drunk when he disappeared. That would make him an easier target," Steve said.

"Bah," Terry said. "It's a stunt, and it's working."

"I don't think so," Lia said. "Didn't you see that clip of his mother on the news? She was hysterical. I can't imagine letting my family think I'd been abducted."

"Verisimilitude," Terry said.

"Cold-hearted," Steve said.

"If that's what it is, she'll never forgive him," Bailey said.

District Five's station house outgrew the quarters assigned to it well before the turn of the millennium. More than a hundred police officers made do with space designed for a squad a third its current size. The building was attractive on the outside, and the parking lot was adequate—especially with the spill-over lot across Ludlow at a now-defunct gas station. For patrol officers it was a minor irritation that lasted as long as roll call in a room that was standing room only.

The detectives suffered like economy passengers on an overseas flight. The District Five bullpen was a long, narrow room with a dozen desks jammed end to end around the perimeter, leaving a narrow space down the middle to navigate. It was a matter of courtesy that no one wore fragrance on the job, and Mexican food was strictly forbidden.

Peter's desk sat at the far end, away from the steady foot traffic near the door. Brent sat around the corner from Peter, having charmed a retiring detective into willing the desk to him in such a way that those who were next in seniority just snorted and let Brent have it.

"Hey Dourson, I heard you were passed over for CID," Hodgkins razzed as he exited the bullpen, followed by his permanent shadow, Jarvis. "You shouldn't let your girlfriend solve your cases for you. Looks bad to the brass."

"I see you're still here," Peter said. "Haven't figured out how to cheat on the I.Q. Test yet?"

Hodgkins shot him the finger and swaggered by.

"When are you going to do something about Hodgkins and his sidekick?" Brent asked as they entered the narrow warren shared by the detectives and headed for their desks. At the moment, the room was uncharacteristically empty.

"You think I should?" Peter asked.

"After they set Brainard on Lia, I was sure you were going to take them down. They've more than earned it."

"True, but the problem with guys like Heckle and Jeckle is, if you retaliate, no one can tell which one of you is the bigger ass."

"So you're doing nothing?" Brent sat back in his chair, arms folded, and stared at Peter in disbelief.

"Oh, ye of little faith. One of the first things they teach in martial arts is to use your opponent's momentum and body weight against him."

"And?"

"When hunting, one waits for the doe to step into the clearing. Timing, Grasshopper, is everything."

Brent shook his head. "So what did Lia say when you told her you were offered a spot in the new homicide division?" Brent asked.

"I didn't tell her and I'm not going to. I already turned it down."

"Brother, say it isn't so. That's a high profile gig with a substantial pay increase. Why would you give it up?"

"High profile, high pressure and lousy hours. I'd be working out of Downtown and going all over the city. Here, I'm away from the politics, I'm close to home, and I only have to acquaint myself with the local losers. I can maintain regular hours and have a personal life."

"Why aren't you telling Lia?"

"She'll think I gave up a good career move for her, and she'll feel pressured."

"Didn't you? Give it up for her?" Brent asked.

"Not exactly. I'm not that ambitious. If we weren't together, I might have taken the slot because I didn't have anything better to do. And the way I understand it, we'll still work cases. We just won't be the guys taking all the heat."

"Smart thinking. And since you're stuck here, you can join me. I got a hot one."

"Oh, really?" Peter asked.

"A precursor of life under the new system. Eighty-three year old woman has called three times this week. She says the neighbor's teen-aged son is beaming weird noises into her house in the middle of the night to make her crazy."

"Can't you just tell her that's impossible?"

"Won't stop her from calling again tomorrow. I promised the desk I'd take a look."

"Five gets you ten it's tinnitus," Peter said.

"You tell her that. See what she says."

"Maybe we can blame it on her dental work."

"First we have to look all over her place for the invisible speakers where these sounds are coming in," Brent said.

"How does she know it's the neighbor's kid? Why isn't it aliens?"

"The young man in question lit fire to a sack of dog doo on her porch when he was eight. Who else would it be?"

"Well, that explains it. Looks like we've got a career criminal to take down."

Sarah looked dubiously at the tether hanging from Lia's belt while she held the door to SCOOP Manor open. "Cecilie's out and it's just us today. You're really going to work with Chewy tied to your side?"

"It's an experiment. Chewy won't focus on me and heel properly. I figure this way, he'll have to."

"That's drastic, isn't it?"

"Desperate times, desperate measures. He's got to be ready for the parade."

Sarah shook her head. "Cats are so much easier."

Lia looked at the row of giant litter boxes to clean and the dozens of milling cats to feed and medicate. "Uh huh, that's why I'm here. Because cats are so easy."

Sarah snorted. "Cats are very easy. That's why it's so easy to wind up with too many of them."

Chewy demonstrated a dangerous interest in the contents of the litter boxes. Sarah settled on scooping while Lia followed with fresh litter, keeping Chewy away from unapproved snacks. The cats soon learned the limits of his tether and took to strolling just beyond his reach. The first fifteen minutes were rough, with Chewy barking constantly while attempting to get a reaction from the cats. Finally he grumbled and took to Lia's side, giving the kitties disgusted looks.

With the noise level back to normal, Lia broached the subject of Leroy's disappearance while they hauled kibble from room to room.

"...so, my resource tracked the pings on the phone. It's been in a number of locations in town. They group around Northside, Saint Bernard, Westwood, and Elmwood. I pinned those neighborhoods on a map for you."

"So he's here?" Sarah asked.

Lia couldn't decipher the expression on Sarah's face. "That's the thing. My, uh, resource can't figure out where Leroy is staying, unless he's sleeping in a car. He can't stay in a motel without leaving a digital footprint, and none of his friends show any changes in activity that suggest they're hiding him. Was that article in *The Huffington Post* today right? The Austin police haven't found anything new?"

"We talked to George Wier yesterday. They think he was smuggled out in a blue van. They can't say for sure because someone threw eggs at the security camera on the loading dock. That left a thirty minute gap in the surveillance videos.

"The guard monitoring the cameras was on an unauthorized break when it happened and it wasn't noticed immediately. He's pleading sudden and explosive diarrhea. It's possible someone pulled the old Visine trick on him.

"Other cameras picked up a Blue van leaving the hotel, but the light was out over the license plate. There are no other leads. We shouldn't know that much, except a couple of the cops are big fans of George's books. You can't tell anyone."

"What's there to tell?" Lia asked. "It's still nothing."

"Sales of the books are going through the roof, and there have been more reported sightings of Lucas Cross than Elvis. If we weren't so worried about Leroy, I'd be celebrating."

"Where are the sightings?" Lia asked.

Sarah flung out an arm while holding a not-quite-empty scoop. Kibble flew across the room, bouncing on the floor. Chewy perked up his ears and chased down the bits he could reach, crunching them before anyone could take them away and tugging on his leash to get to the ones beyond the extent of his tether. A trio of kitties sat just beyond his limits, blandly munching on kibble. Chewy whined.

"Oops. At least we don't have to worry about picking it up. Reports are from all over. Bangor. Joshua Tree. Cabo San Lobos. Sydney. None from Belize."

Lia took a deep breath. "My, uh, resource, sometimes sees things."

"Sees things?'

"Like a psychic."

"Oh?" Sarah seemed interested. "Does he have spirit guides and go into trances?"

"I don't know how it works, or even if it does work. He says he saw Leroy confined to an air-conditioned box in the middle of a wasteland, and Leroy was happy."

Sarah spewed, spraying spit, and doubled over laughing. She attempted to talk, but shook her head, gasping instead. Sarah sat on the kibble bin, head in her hands as her gasps turned into sobs.

Lia, never comfortable with strong emotion, was at a loss. Chewy gave Sarah a puzzled look and nudged her knee until she gave in and patted his head. Finally she straightened up.

"Sorry, it's just so typical. Leroy, stuck in a wasteland? As in, he's happy being in a drunken stupor? That's brilliant. It would explain why he hasn't come home. ... I shouldn't laugh. It's just, that would be Leroy's idea of the good life. Wouldn't matter if he had a box, or if he slept under a tree. Still, it doesn't explain where he is, does it?"

Lia made a wry face. "No, it doesn't."

"Don't ask your 'resource' about me. I'm afraid of what he'd say." Sarah wiped her hands on her pants and stood up, resolute. She picked up the scoop and returned to shoveling kibble. "I'm not sharing this with Debby. It would just send her into a tirade. I can hear her in my head, as it is."

"Sorry," Lia said. "Where does this leave Carol? How is she doing, anyway?"

Sarah grimaced. "She's jumpy. She won't go out at night, though that's a moot point while her leg is banged up. She can't drive."

"If it isn't Leroy, who do you suppose it is?" Lia asked.

"The pings put him here, whatever he told Alice. I didn't want to believe he'd hurt anyone, but I can't believe that he's in town and not connected to the attack on Carol. I'm so glad you and Peter were there to help her."

"You really think Leroy would hurt any of you?"

Sarah sighed. "Leroy ... he always liked the idea of an easy score, and he's not a mastermind. That's why playing Lucas Cross was perfect for him."

"But what would the point be? What could he get out of hurting Carol?"

"I don't know. She's our accountant. Maybe money is involved."

"Can't you convince her to go to the police?"

"Not at this point. We need to find Leroy ourselves and figure out a way to bring him home that will keep us all out of trouble. But we can't look for him, he'd see us coming.

"Private detective?"

"Do you know one that wouldn't sell the story? That you'd trust your entire future with? Because we sure don't."

"I see what you mean."

"Exactly. I was hoping you and your friends could look into it."

"What, *precisely*, did Alma tell you about me?"

"That if she were in trouble, she'd trust you and Peter to sort it out. We can't use Peter, so that leaves you."

Lia sighed. *I'll never get back to my painting.* "I don't work alone. I don't have the skills. I'm not promising anything, but I'll get the gang together and we'll discuss it."

"I knew you were hiding something," Terry said with a fierce certainty that reinforced his resemblance to Teddy Roosevelt.

Lia scanned the faces in her living room. Every set of eyes, both canine and human, was on her. *How do I wind up in these situations?*

"It wasn't mine to share until I had the go-ahead," she explained.

"And now that you want footwork done, you're bringing the peons in?" Steve asked, head tilted at a skeptical angle honed by years of negotiating for the sewer workers union.

"Hey, no call to be mean," Jose said. "If Lia couldn't say anything, she couldn't say anything." He leaned down to scratch Sophie's boulder head. "Mean people suck, don't they, Sophie?"

Sophie panted at Fleece, who panted back.

Lia looked at Jim. "Are you mad at me, too?"

Jim shrugged. "It's just gossip until it has something to do with me. Now it has something to do with me, and you told us."

"It's not that I want anything done. We've been asked to help in a very touchy situation. I'm not crazy about it. I can't tell Peter, and I hate that. I want to know what you want to do."

"Do we get anything out of this?" Steve asked.

"Pennies in Heaven?" Bailey suggested.

"You want to profit from their troubles?" Jim asked quietly.

Even in shorts and a tee shirt, he still looks like an old testament prophet. Or a saint.

"Just asking," Steve said. "There's a lot of money in play. Isn't that what this is about? That has to be worth something."

"I never thought about it," Lia said. "I don't know how much money they really have. Most of it goes to animal rescue organizations."

"What do you want?" Bailey held out her elegant hands, palms up. "We need to figure out what to ask for."

"Aw geez," Jose said. "I don't wanna take money away from stray cats."

"When you put it that way, it starts to sound like taking bread from nuns," Steve said.

"I don't like cats," Jim said, dispelling the illusion of sainthood. "Do they help dogs, too?"

"I'm sure they do," Lia said.

"Then I vote we help them. I don't want anything," Jim said.

Bailey cocked a brow at Terry.

"It would be unchivalrous to expect anything," he said.

"Are we all in?" Lia asked.

"I'm new to this," Steve said. "Do we have a group hug now, or what?"

"What we do," Lia said, is figure out how we're going to find Leroy. And we do it before Peter's baseball game is over."

"The Reds aren't playing tonight," Steve said.

"Peter's on the District Five team," Bailey said. "How long do you think we have?"

Lia looked at the clock, calculating. "We should have at least an hour." She picked up her phone and tapped a message. "That's for insurance."

"What did you do?" Bailey asked.

"I sent a text reminding Peter to stop at the store on the way over. Since I never asked him to pick up anything, he'll have to call me to find out what I want."

"Smart thinkin'," Jose said.

"I'll have to go to confession when this is over, and I'm not even Catholic," Lia said.

"It's for a good cause," Jim said.

"What's the plan?" Jose asked.

Lia opened her laptop computer to display a map of Cincinnati cell phone coverage. The map was overlaid with transparent blue circles containing dates.

"The blue areas are pings from Leroy's burner phone. If you look at the dates, the most frequent pings are in Elmwood and Westwood."

"That's a big area. How do you expect to find him?" Steve asked.

"I haven't a clue," Lia said.

79

The group sat, stumped.

"People are creatures of habit," Jim said. "What are his habits?"

"Everyone says this guy likes to hang out in bars and bullshit," Steve said.

"He can't risk places like Northside Tavern or The Comet, because people would recognize him," Lia said. "I think he'd pick little Westside bars that cater to older residents, folks who don't have internet."

"We goin' bar hoppin'?" Jose asked. "'Cause I don't drink."

"You're a born and bred Westsider," Bailey said. "You know they don't like outsiders. You'd be most convincing of all of us to walk into those little bars and get the regulars talking."

"If you ordered your beer in cans, no one would know how much you actually drank except the bartender when he tosses it away," Terry said. "And then you'd be gone."

"I need a date. Which one of you ladies is going to be my date?"

"I guess Bailey and I can take turns," Lia said. "Are you up for this, Bailey?"

"If it doesn't go on too late. I get up at five."

"We're all getting up early for parade practice," Steve said.

"We need at least two teams or this will take forever," Jim said.

"Terry, you can't go. You're sure to run into someone who flunked out of Alcoholics Anonymous and knows you don't belong in a bar. Jim's out," Bailey said.

"Why am I out?" he asked, affronted. "I can fake drinking a beer."

"You don't have the right personality for bar hopping. I don't think Bonnie would like it, either," Lia said. "And there's something else that only you can do. Steve?"

"Sure, why not. A Westside bar will be a piece of cake after the sewers and the Homeless Association."

"Then we can split up. I'll go with Jose, and Bailey, you can go with Steve. That way, each team will have a native on it."

"I'm on call tomorrow, can we do this Wednesday?" Jose asked.

"That would be better," Lia said. "Steve? Bailey?"

At their nods, she turned to Terry. "Can you come up with a list of bars near the pings? I'll email you a copy of the map. Check the times. Pings after eight p.m. are most important."

"What am I, chopped liver?" Jim asked.

"You surveyed half the buildings in those neighborhoods. I'd like to send you the map and just have you study it to see if it suggests anything to you, what Leroy is doing in those areas when he's not drinking, where he might be hiding."

Lia's cell phone chimed.

"That's Peter." She checked the screen and tapped out a return text.

The group rustled. The dogs sense imminent departure and stretched, yawning. Lia counted tea glasses. *Dammit. Better wash those.*

"What did you ask him to bring?" Bailey asked, snapping a lead on Kita's collar.

"Almond milk. What else?"

Chapter 5

Wednesday, June 22

Cecilie took a slug of her pre-swim energy drink and bundled her unruly hair under a bathing cap. *Acai berry, my ass. The closest this stuff ever came to fruit was … No, don't think about that. Why do they have to sweeten it so damn much? How old do they think I am, four?*

"Hey, gorgeous." Edward sat down on the lounger next to hers. He retained a shadow of the good looks he had as a young man and was overly proud of his 60-going-on-55 year-old physique. Perversely, his lecherous tendencies grew as his attractiveness waned. Now that his doctor would not allow him to drink, he haunted the pool at Twin Towers Retirement Center, the only indoor pool in the area.

Cecilie tried to be good natured about Edward's flirting, what else could you do, except ruin your own day? This morning her back was acting up more than usual and she didn't have the patience. She desperately wanted to punch him in the throat. Today he wore his American flag Speedos. Cecilie figured he had a different pair for every day of the week. Anything to get the widows at Twin Towers looking at his package. What there was of it.

"Edward, if you're talking to me, you need your prescription checked. I'm no more gorgeous than you are charming."

Edward pouted. "Can't a man flatter a pretty woman in a bathing suit? You didn't use to be so mean."

"No, I wasn't. Before I got mean, I was stupid. And that was thirty years ago. Thirty very long years that have warped your memory. It didn't happen then, it isn't going to happen now, and don't bother pretending that it might. Now go on. I have to do my physical therapy."

Somehow, that man is going to turn our conversation around so that he's convinced I can't get enough of him. Ugh. Damn back. Well, the sooner I get swimming, the sooner it will loosen up.

Cecilie's spine had been fused in surgery several years earlier. She figured she was carrying a pound of titanium screws in her vertebrae. *18 vertebrae, each with two screws, 36 screws. More like two or three pounds.* One of these days she'd find out how much a titanium screw weighed and do the math. Daily swimming was the only thing that kept the pain within bounds. She still had to take massive doses of pain killers just to feel normal. *And if I don't feel normal, cleaning litter boxes is hell.*

Cecilie took one last swallow of the hated energy drink and set the bottle at the side of the pool. She tugged the straps of her racing bathing suit in place and walked down the steps into the water, ignoring the chill as it rose up over her calves and thighs. She took a shallow dive to immerse herself before swimming over to the far left lane.

This was a single lane that she liked to commandeer for herself. The other three lanes were double lanes that had to be shared. The backstroke was easiest on her spine, but she kicked up enough water to drown a mermaid. So, she kept to the solo lane out of politeness and concern for public safety. That, and she had difficulty navigating on her back. She couldn't see where she was going. If she shared a lane, she was likely to ram her titanium reinforced body into the other swimmer.

Her lane hogging had not endeared her to others at the fitness center. For some reason the snotty receptionist, Janet, objected to her desire to keep the lane for herself even though it was only big enough for one person to use at a time. She looked up to see Janet glaring at her over the strings of buoys marking the lanes. *To hell with her. I'll be in here for less than thirty minutes. Wait till her body falls apart, and see how she feels about needing a little consideration.*

Cecilie turned on her back and began slowly stroking her way across the pool, gradually speeding up as her muscles warmed and relaxed. She fell into the rhythm, stroking to the far side of the pool, pushing off for the return lap.

The 12th lap, time for a break. She pulled herself up at the side of the pool, grabbed her water bottle, and finished off her energy drink. A few minutes to catch her breath, and it was time for two laps of the breast stroke. Her version of the breast stroke was all arms so she could rest her legs. Face down in the water, she began to drift in her mind, and to relax. the relaxation became deeper than she expected. A fog came on her, her eyes drifting shut against her will as she struggled against the lead in her arms. When she started to sink, she no longer had the awareness to panic.

The first thing Cecilie noticed was the chill of air on her skin and something thumping her back as she lay on her side. She must be laying on concrete, it was cold and hard and scraped her skin. She convulsed and vomited a combination of pool water and acai drink onto the pool apron. As she continued coughing, the hand began soothing circles. It took all her effort to slit her eyes open. Three pairs of feet lined up before her, two in pumps and the other large, masculine and barefoot.

Someone, the only someone who was actually doing anything, propped her up. Cecile twisted around to see Alice kneeling beside her, concern on her face. She turned back and identified the feet as belonging to Edward, Janet, and the director of the fitness center.

"What happened to you?" Alice asked. "I walked in and you were floating facedown in the water. Edward pulled you out. We thought you had a heart attack."

"I suppose you called for an ambulance," Cecilie rasped, resigning herself to hours of prodding under harsh fluorescent lights.

"It's standard procedure, Cecilie," the director said. "Liability issues, you know."

"I didn't have a heart attack," Cecilie said. "I just became very sleepy and passed out. I don't understand what happened."

"That shouldn't have occurred," Alice said. "Have you changed medications lately? Had any dizzy spells? Blood sugar issues?"

Cecilie shook her head to all of Alice's suggestions.

"What about your pain meds? Any chance you double dosed yourself this morning?"

Cecilie laughed, then winced in pain. "If I had done that, I wouldn't have made it into the pool."

Firemen arrived before the ambulance. Soon a surreal committee stood conferring over Cecilie, annoying her to no end while they went through the the process of reaching a forgone conclusion. She would have to go to the hospital.

Many tests and fruitless hours after Cecilie's arrival at Good Sam, no cause had been assigned to her loss of consciousness. The doctors shrugged their shoulders and said the mechanisms of fainting had not been thoroughly studied, and they did not know what the answer was. One obliquely suggested an eating disorder might be responsible. Cecilie looked the intern in the eye and said, "Get real. With *this* body?"

A timid young aide waited until the doctors and nurses were gone and tentatively asked if she'd had anything to drink before she went in the pool.

"I had my water bottle with me," Cecilie responded. "Why do you ask?"

"Just water?" The aide tilted her head as if that would help her peer into Cecilie's brain.

"I always put energy powder in it before I swim."

"I'm just an aide. I'm not a doctor, but I couldn't help overhearing. It sounded like something that happened to a girlfriend of mine in a bar. This guy roofied her. Good thing my boyfriend and I showed up before he could get her out the door."

Cecilie and Alice exchanged glances.

Cecilie and Alice sat in the back room of Sidewinder Coffee with cappuccinos and chocolate croissants.

"What a miserable waste of time and insurance," Cecilie sighed. "Thank you for getting me out of there. I hate hospitals. What were you doing at Twin Towers?"

"I thought you might like to get lunch." Alice looked at her watch. "Too late for that now."

"Oh, well. This is all I can handle right now anyway."

"I keep thinking about what that aide told us," Alice said.

"About roofies? That makes no sense."

"It wouldn't have to be roofies. Any sedative would do. Did your energy drink taste different today?"

"I try not to taste it. Stuff's nasty. It could have anything in it. You think someone drugged me? For what purpose?"

"Why did Leroy disappear? Why did someone shove Carol down the steps?" Alice asked.

"I get your point. Though it could have been Edward. I could see him doing it so he could play hero. Maybe Janet did it so I'd stop swimming in her pool. It might have nothing to do with anything else."

"Who had access to your water bottle?"

Cecilie shrugged. "Could have been anyone. It was sitting by the side of the pool while I was swimming. I don't think anyone messed with it there, they would have been seen. But I keep it in the car, and the car is usually unlocked."

"You don't lock your car?"

"Too many young punks breaking into cars around here. I'd rather let them in so they can see I have nothing of value than deal with a broken window."

Alice sighed. "Good thing the others are on their way. We have to talk about this."

Sarah walked in, followed by Carol. They took the empty seats at Cecilie's table. "We have to make this quick. I've got exactly 17 minutes before I have to be on the circulation desk, and it will take five minutes to walk back. Alice, you're taking Carol home."

"What about Debby?" Alice asked.

"Staff meeting," Sarah said. "She can't get away. We'll have to fill her in later."

"We have to sniff your car," Carol said.

"What on earth for?" Cecilie asked.

"I caught a whiff of Dunhill right before I was pushed," Carol said. "I can't imagine any other idiot around here paying $250 a bottle for cologne. If we smell it in your car, it proves Leroy was involved."

"What about your water bottle?" Alice asked. "We should have it tested."

"By who?" Carol demanded. "We can't go to the police with this."

"Where is your bottle, Cecilie?" Sarah asked.

Alice and Cecilie looked at each other.

"We must have left it at Twin Towers," Cecilie admitted. "You didn't get it, did you, Alice?"

Alice shook her head. "I grabbed your towel. I didn't think about the bottle. Maybe they kept it for you."

"And maybe they threw it in the trash," Sarah said. "This is getting us nowhere. I can't believe Leroy is stalking us. He's an idiot, but he's Debby's idiot."

The others stared at her.

Sarah shrugged. "Debby couldn't be here, so I'm acting as her proxy."

"You didn't hear him during our last rehearsal," Carol said. "He was furious when I refused to support his bid for more money. I'm not surprised he's taken matters into his own hands."

"So he's going to kill the goose?" Alice asked.

"When you've got a gaggle of geese, what's one or two?" Cecilie asked.

"He hasn't been successful in killing anyone yet. Maybe he just means to scare us," Sarah said.

"Or maybe he's just incompetent," Cecilie said.

"He's got us over a barrel," Carol said. "He knows we can't go to the police."

"Or maybe he's dead," Alice said. "We don't know for a fact it was him."

"I know what I smelled," Carol said.

"You didn't see him clearly," Alice said. "Anyone can wear cologne."

"From now on," Sarah said, "we buddy up. No one goes anywhere alone until we figure this out."

"Oh, wonderful," Cecilie said. "Why don't we just get one of those loopy ropes they use with kindergarteners. We'll go everywhere together. That will keep us safe."

"Are you going to be that person?" Sarah asked Cecilie.

"What person do you mean?"

"The dead person whose last brilliant idea was to investigate a strange noise without her ball bat. There's at least one in every horror movie."

"Why a ball bat?" Cecilie asked.

"I don't like guns. You know that."

"Ball bat it is, then," Cecilie said.

"Sarah, what do you think is driving this?" Alice asked.

"I don't think it's coming from Leroy. I don't think he cares about the big picture, as long as he gets to be the bad boy author with adoring female fans. Someone else would have to be pushing him."

"According to Debby, he never was much of a go-getter," Alice said.

"This farce required serious go-getting," Sarah said.

"You know who makes the least sense in this whole thing?" Cecilie asked.

"Who's that?" Alice asked.

"That Citrine girl," Cecilie said, eyes narrowing. "She claims she and Leroy are soulmates on that blog of hers. Debby doesn't know who she is, Dorothy doesn't know who she is, and Leroy's friends don't either."

Chapter 6

"Did you have any luck last night?" Parade practice over, Bailey climbed up next to Lia on their usual table. Their dogs raced off, happy to be done with school for the day. Lia watched as the rest of their group headed down the service road to their cars, some headed for work, others for appointments.

"Ha, ha. I nearly floated away on club soda by the time Jose and I were done. We hit seven bars in three hours. Nobody reacted to Leroy's picture, except one woman who claimed he was her old high school sweetheart and wanted his number. She didn't get the concept that we were looking for him."

"Such a shame."

"Don't feel too sorry for her. She couldn't remember his name, and she was about a decade too old to be in his graduating class."

"What did you wind up telling Peter?"

"I said I was modeling details on the gun and I had to keep at it, or the Bondo would separate later."

"Good thinking. Is there Bondo on the float?"

"There will be by tonight."

"Oops. Steve and I didn't do any better. We also stopped in at the local pony kegs, in case he was buying his beer and taking it somewhere else. I don't get it. Trees sent me last night's pings, and Leroy was somewhere in Elmwood Place. That neighborhood shuts down by nine, except for the places we went. So where was he? I even tried calling his phone in case he was nearby. I thought we might get lucky and hear it ringing."

"What would you have done if he answered?" Lia asked.

"Asked him where he was, of course. It just went to voicemail. But why is his phone on? He's not making calls."

Lia shook her head. "I don't know. Debby says he doesn't read, so maybe he doesn't realize he can be tracked that way. I talked to Sarah. Now they'd like us to take a look at Citrine to see if she's involved in some way."

"At least we'll be able to find her," Bailey said, looking out across the dog park. "What do you plan to do? And when are you taking Chewy to the vet? He's still eating dirt."

Lia scowled down at Chewy, who had propped his forelegs on the picnic table bench and was grinning at her, his teeth white against his mud-stained muzzle. She twisted her mouth.

"We went. He's perfectly healthy. The vet tells me there used to be a horse stable on this site, and he expects most of the dogs find the flavor irresistible. All that manure. I can either muzzle him, get the park board to relocate us, or forget about it."

"Yuck. You still let him kiss you?"

"I try not to think about it. As for Citrine, I think a ruse is in order. She obviously wants media attention. We'll offer to give her some."

"How are we going to do that?" Bailey asked.

"We need to find a blog, something that would be attractive to her, that doesn't have photos of its contributors. One of us will pretend to be one of the writers and interview her."

"Sounds complicated and time consuming. You need to keep it simple. How about this? You're college buddies with a contributor to some hot blog and since they knew you were part of the Lucas Cross machine, they tapped you for a piece on how his disappearance is affecting the home front."

"That's brilliant, Bailey. Maybe you should interview her."

"I'm 48. Most bloggers are half my age. Besides, while you're meeting with her, Terry and I can steal her garbage. We can dig through it for clues. We might even be able to break into her apartment."

"Isn't house-breaking against the New Age creed?"

"My heart is pure. I seek only to learn, not take."

"You're taking this seriously," Lia said.

"Citrine will be on her best behavior when you interview her. You can only find out so much from what people are willing to make public. We need to dig—and I mean that literally—deeper. It's the only way to find out if she's helping Lucas."

"What if you break in and Lucas is there?"

"Call 911. What do you think I'm going to do—take his picture and post it on Facebook?"

Lia sighed. "Looks like I'm going to spend the morning pawing through her blog."

"Once was enough angst for me. I'd rather see her garbage."

Chapter 7

Melt Cafe was a vegan-friendly deli that frequently served organic food. The small front dining room featured lavender walls. Magnetic poetry sets were mounted on the walls at table level so patrons could amuse themselves while they waited for their orders. Above the poetry sets, neighborhood artists exhibited their work.

A narrow hallway led past the counter and kitchen to the rear dining room. Vintage tables and chairs of various styles provided seating, while the walls were painted in wavy vertical stripes in new millennium decorator colors.

Lia passed out the back door onto a gravel patio, a feature of most Northside restaurants. Melt's patio had a rabbit hutch. She stooped in front of the chicken-wire cage and its lone occupant. *What's your name, little guy? Do you know Alice's bunny, Bugs? Do you have amorous designs on shoes?*

Lia waved from her table when Citrine entered the back patio. Lia recognized her by her hair, artfully waifish and streaked with varying shades of orange and yellow, with a hint of red, shocking against pale skin and gray clothes.

Citrine flashed a smile of recognition and joined her, extending her arm for a limp handshake.

"Love your hair," Lia said, discretely tapping the send button on her phone, then activating the recording app.

"Thanks. Taylor Jameson did it. It's nice to meet you," Citrine said.

Citrine hung her hobo bag on the back of a chair, claiming a seat on the shaded side of the umbrella table. *Good thing. She's got to be sweltering in Doc Martins and tights.* Closer inspection revealed an abundance of gray cat hair on her tunic. *What are those sleeves hiding? Embarrassing ink? Track marks? Cutting scars?*

Citrine's build was very slim and fragile, what some folks in the goth/paranormal world called "fairy." *Or is it Emo? I can never tell the difference. Anorexic? Bulimic? I'll know when she orders.*

"I'm so glad you agreed to meet with me," Lia said. "Please, order anything. I'm buying."

"Oh, I'm not hungry," Citrine said. "I'll have some raspberry iced tea."

Breatharian, then. Well, I'm going to pretend rye bread doesn't have wheat in it and splurge. "I hope you don't mind if I have a sandwich," Lia said.

"Oh, not at all."

Lia flagged down a waitress and ordered the Rachel, a turkey rueben with a hipster twist, and two of the herbal iced teas.

"So, you're an artist, too. I don't know if you noticed the paintings out front. I'm the featured artist here this month."

Lia recalled listless blobs of color overlaid with text and cryptic ink drawings. "Yes, very nice. I especially liked the blue one with the mermaid and the boar."

"'Gored in Love.' Most people think it's a pig. They don't get the difference. That's my favorite. The ocean is so evocative, don't you think? Sensuous and deadly. It represents my relationship with Leroy—you do know Lucas's real name is Leroy, don't you?"

Bingo. "Yes, Leroy Eberschlag."

"It's German, you know? Eber means 'boar' and schlag means 'strike'. So it's like being gored by a boar. That's how it feels, having Leroy ripped away from me." Citrine sniffed, dabbing gently at her nose with a paper napkin.

"I'm so sorry. Is this hard to talk about?"

"A little, but it helps, you know?"

Like spilling your guts all over the internet helps. "I've read your poems and your blog, but you never mention where you met Leroy. Is this something you can talk about?"

"Oh, but I do. In 'Slice by Slice,' the first poem I wrote about him. It's a double entendre. Pain and pizza. I work at the Pizza place around the corner, the one that sells slices of pizza through a window after the bars close. He used to come all the time."

"And how did you get started?"

"With Leroy?" Citrine ducked her head and glanced sideways at Lia. "He used to come by with his friends,

Dave and Orin. This handsome guy who teased me and called me Hot Stuff, you know, because of my hair."

She smiled sadly and angled her head, looking off as if she could see through the privacy fence and into some misty distance.

"One night he was by himself and he just looked at me and didn't say anything. He looked so far into me, like he could see down to my toes. All I could do was stare back. We were seeing all the way through each other. It was spiritual. I didn't know who he was. I mean, I knew he wrote, but everyone writes. I didn't know he was Lucas Cross. Then his picture was all over the internet and he was gone. Now I don't know if we'll ever be together again."

Translation: He showed up drunk at the pizza window when she was closing up and she invited him in for leftover pizza and a blow job. If her boss ever found out, she'd be fired.

"You don't mention Leroy on your blog before he disappeared. When did you get together?"

"I don't remember the date ..."

Liar.

"But it was still so new, I wasn't ready to make it public."

Meaning he forgot about it right after it happened. Maybe he was in a brownout.

"When he disappeared, well, I felt like my soul was being ripped apart. I couldn't stop writing or painting. It was the only way to deal, you know?"

Lia's sandwich arrived. Citrine swallowed hard and looked away from Lia's demolition of animal flesh, chattering about the media requests she'd gotten since she started posting about Leroy on her blog.

"...Until you emailed me, it was just the regional press and some small blogs that were interested in my story, you know, public-access cable shows and stuff. But *Huffington Post*, that's awesome-sauce. Who else are you interviewing?"

Lia washed down a bite of her sandwich. "I don't know yet. I think it might be too intrusive to talk to his mother right now. His aunt Debby might give me the family picture since I know her."

Citrine scowled and leaned forward, confidential. "I hope she's not a good friend of yours. She's been so rude to me since this happened."

"Oh?"

"She called me a twit when I went by to, you know, offer my support. They aren't the only ones who lost him."

"You went to see Debby? What happened?"

"She was with somebody and they were fighting. The front window was open, so I could hear it. I was going to leave, but I guess she saw me through the window. Debby yanks the door open and yells 'Get out of here, you ignorant twit' and slams the door in my face."

"That's awful! What do you suppose they were arguing about?"

Citrine stirred her tea. "I didn't catch much, just somebody saying, 'why would I lie about something like that' and Debby saying, 'I won't believe it until I hear it myself. Oh, wait, I can't'. She was really snarky."

"Do you have any idea what they were talking about?"

"Not a clue."

"When was this?"

Citrine pursed her lips as she mentally counted back. "Not long after they returned to town. June 15th or 16th, I think."

"Have you talked to his friends?"

"Dave and Orin?" This time the scowl was darker. "They offered to *console* me. *Together.* I don't want to talk about them. He was their friend, and they *hit* on me."

"You said you didn't know Leroy was Lucas Cross, but you knew he was a writer. What did he tell you about his writing?"

Citrine's eyes grew dreamy. "He said he was going to make me a heroine in one of his novels, a woman of fire and spirit who would save the world."

"And you never read one of his books?"

"He promised to let me read something, but he disappeared. When I found out who he was, I tried to read *Koi*, but it was too violent. I think he found inspiration in me to try something more spiritual. Profound."

Her eyes drooped in what Lia thought of as a Pre-Raphaelite languor. *Obviously born too late, and on the wrong continent. What is she on? She's got to be making this up.*

Citrine sighed. "We may never know."

Bailey counted the houses as Terry drove down the brick alley behind Fergus Avenue. The street consisted of pre-World War II shotgun homes converted into multi-unit dwellings. They approached one with a tiny back yard and space for four cars to pull in. A quartet of city-mandated rolling garbage bins sat by the curb, their lids still closed. Each was spray painted with the address and unit number to deter theft.

"It's that one, the three-story brick painted four shades of blue. Guess the owner couldn't decide what color to go with."

"Perhaps he used discounted paint and went with what they had."

"Cheap landlords. What can you do?"

Terry pulled up by the bins. "Check her mailbox, see what unit she's in."

Bailey hopped out of John's truck and made her way to the side, where a hodgepodge of mailboxes were mounted on the side. She bee-lined for one painted virulent swirls of orange and hit pay dirt.

"Number 2," she said as she joined Terry. "Let's grab our boxes."

It took less than three minutes to load Citrine's garbage bags into the back of Terry's truck. He drove around the corner and parked.

"What do you think?" Terry asked. "Shall we undertake entry?"

"She's on the ground floor and her door is on the side. We can check it out without being noticed."

"Too bad we don't have heat sensing equipment. It would be better to know if there's anyone in there now."

"I have a low tech version," Bailey said.

"Really? Do tell!"

"We knock."

Terry examined the lock while Bailey rapped on the door. When there was no response, Terry took out his wallet and extracted his library card. He examined the back to ensure he wouldn't damage the magnetic strip, then slid it in the gap between the door and the jamb. One quick jerk up and forward, and the door popped open.

"Idiot landlord should be shot for not installing deadbolts. Doesn't he know this is a drug ridden neighborhood?" Shaking his head, Terry examined the card before he put it back in his wallet. "A little dinged, but still functional. Shall we?"

Bailey handed him a pair of neoprene gloves. Belatedly, he wiped his fingerprints off the doorknob with his shirttail.

"We need to be in and out," Bailey said quietly. "Just take pictures of everything and we can figure out what it means later. Don't disturb anything."

A grey, long-haired cat larger than any Bailey had ever seen, strolled out and meowed loudly. It had pumpkin colored eyes.

"Must be where Citrine gets her color scheme."

"Aw. Cute kitty," Terry said, leaning down to pet it.

It hissed and arched its back, revealing sharp, raptor teeth.

"That's not a cat," Bailey said. "That's a demonic presence. Leave it alone. I'm not going to retrieve your soul from hell if it bites you."

"Good advice."

Bailey looked around. Paintings on paper were tacked all over the walls. "Get pictures of all the art. I'll shoot her bedroom."

"The lass seems to go for quantity over quality," Terry said, "though there is a certain evocative sensibility."

"Yeah, she took a correspondence course from the guy who painted big-eyed girls."

"If I'm not mistaken, Walter Keane took credit for his wife's paintings. A feminazi like yourself should know that," Terry called after Bailey as she left the room.

"Whatever." Bailey opened the closet door to find a half dozen identical grey tunics hanging over several pairs of mannish, lace-up shoes and boots. More colorful clothing was jammed to the side. "No evidence of male occupation," she told Terry as he wandered in.

"By Jove, what is this?" Terry said.

"What?" Bailey turned and faced a wall full of sketches she assumed to be Leroy.

"Is this the shrine of an obsessed stalker?" Terry asked.

"Plenty of artists are obsessed with their subjects. Doesn't make them stalkers."

"Something creepy about these."

Bailey took another look. "I don't know. It's self-consciously emo creepy, not Ricardo Lopez crazy. She still has stuffed animals. Now, if Pooh Bear had a kitchen knife in his gut, I'd feel differently. Keep your eye out for signs she's making acid bombs, just in case."

She took pictures of the array of bottles and trinkets on the dresser. "Shoot the food in her fridge and her kitchen cabinets, I'll get the bathroom. Then we need to get out of here." She checked her phone. "We've been here much too long."

"Won't Lia text us when Citrine leaves?"

"And if she forgets?"

"Aye, Aye, Captain."

Bathroom surveyed, Bailey returned to the living room to see Terry tapping a password into an iPad.

"Terry, don't—"

Terry looked up at her as he hit the last digit.

A waitress was removing Lia's empty plate when a police siren sounded from Citrine's phone.

"Will you excuse me?" Citrine asked. "That's an emergency notification."

She tapped her phone, then stared.

"Is something wrong?" Lia asked.

"There's someone in my apartment. I've got to call the police. Sorry, but I have to go." Citrine shoved her chair back. The weight of her hobo bag pulled the chair over. It landed in the gravel. The hobo bag spilled its contents.

"Dammit! Of all the stupid—Call 911 for me, will you?"

Hell, no!

"You call, I'll get your things." Lia dropped onto the gravel, mindless of the pain, and grabbed up make up cases, a scattering of colored pens, and a brocade change purse. She was reaching for a stack of folded paper when Citrine crouched down, phone to her ear, and said, "That's all right, I've got this. ... No, I was talking to someone else. Yes, I'm less than five minutes away. I'll meet the police there." She hauled the bag over her shoulder and strode out, the phone still to her ear.

Once Citrine's back was turned, Lia called Bailey. *Pick up, pick up, pick up ...*

"What is it?"

"Abort! Get the hell out of there!"

Lia held her door open as Bailey and Terry carried their bags of trash up the walk.

"Take it out back, will you? We can look at it on the picnic table."

Chewy, tethered to Lia, tagged along. Sensing some new game, Honey followed.

"What the hell happened?" Lia asked.

"What do you mean?" Terry asked, blinking like Hugh Grant.

Lia looked at Bailey. "Is he serious? How did Citrine know you broke into her apartment? She was on the phone with the police when I called you. You're lucky you got out of there in time."

"Mr. Mensa IQ, here, decided to break into Citrine's iPad."

"Don't you know they turn into a brick if you enter the wrong code too many times?" Lia glared at Terry. "Then she'd know someone had been there."

Terry looked affronted. "I do know, and it takes six failed log-ins. I planned to stop at five."

"Too bad," Bailey drawled, "it only takes three to trigger the security app. It takes a picture of the person trying to break in and sends it to the owner."

"Genius move, Terry," Lia said. "Now the police have your picture. How will I explain that to Peter?"

"I think we may be okay. I turned my head at the critical moment. If we're lucky, all they have is a blur of my very hairy ear," Terry said.

"I hope so," Lia grumbled.

"You know," Bailey said, "since you were there when Citrine called the police, it would be natural for you to call her to find out what happened. She's never seen Terry, so she won't know you're connected."

"Or we can wait for her to blog about it," Lia said, sighing. "If I call her, next thing you know, I'll be her new best friend and she'll feel free to hound me about *The Huffington Post*. That's the last thing I want."

"Sorry," Bailey said.

Lia nodded toward the bags. "What do we have?"

They untied the bags. Bailey handed out neoprene gloves and they removed the contents, piece by piece.

Citrine's diet ran heavily to Ramen noodles. She discarded the flavor packets, suggesting she was vegan, or perhaps paranoid about chemicals. Discarded drawings indicated a good eye and an insecure hand, as well as a tendency to be self-critical.

"Do you suppose she re-writes her blog as many times as she restarts her drawings?" Bailey asked.

"I don't know, but it's likely."

"Her bills are addressed to Cheryl Baremore," Terry said. "That must be her real name."

"Hair chalk wrappers," Lia snorted. "She said Taylor Jameson did her hair."

"Maybe she did the first time, and Citrine keeps it up herself?" Bailey suggested.

"Why lie about it? If I could do my hair like that—I wouldn't, but if I could, I'd sure let people know."

The review of Citrine's garbage and the photos of her belongings revealed nothing more than her life as a cultural edge dweller with a desperate desire to be somebody— the hot artist/internet blogger engaging in a dubious grand passion with a semi-famous writer.

Bailey looked at the photos again. "You know, we've been looking at what's there. We haven't been looking at what's not there."

"What do you mean?" Terry asked. "We know there's nothing that suggests contact with Leroy. If I had gotten into her iPad, we would know conclusively."

"We don't need her email or her texts," Bailey said. "What we don't have are any gifts or detritus from Leroy. *If* she were in love with him and *if* she spent any time at all around him, she'd have something with a bit of Lucas Cross juju on it, even if it was a cigarette butt."

"Oh," Lia said. "Like in *Emma,* her friend who made a treasure out of a bit of gauze she trimmed off when she bandaged the minister's finger."

"Exactly," Bailey said. "Or like Monica Lewinsky, who never dry cleaned that dress after it got Clinton's DNA on it."

"I would say that's taking sentiment to a revolting degree," Terry said.

"It may be history, but it's still disgusting," Lia said.

"She'd at least have access to his pizza garbage," Lia said. "Where's the napkin that pressed against the lips of Lucas Cross?"

"What conclusion do you draw from this observation?" Terry asked.

"Either she's making the whole thing up," Bailey said.

"Or Leroy was nobody to her until she found out he was Lucas and he was in the news, and she's either convinced herself that she has this grand passion—" Lia said.

"Or she's using what little contact she's had with him to further her virtual presence," Bailey concluded.

Terry stared at them. "No wonder I've been divorced four times. It's not that I don't understand women, it's that you truly are incomprehensible."

Chapter 8

Monday, June 27

Peter glanced up from his computer to see Cal Hinkle standing hesitantly by the door. He waved the freckled young officer over.

"This may not be important, but I thought Brent should see my report on a break in that happened last Friday."

Brent swiveled around. "Someone stealing swimwear from the Swedish Bikini Team? I'm all ears."

"No, sir. Someone broke into the apartment of a young lady who has a connection with Leroy Eberschlag. I don't know if it's connected, but I thought I should call it to your attention since you're the official liaison."

"Hawt dayum." Though fragrance was forbidden in the bullpen, it was hard not to smell magnolias whenever the Georgia transplant spoke. "Let's hear it."

"911 received a call from Cheryl Baremore shortly after noon on Friday. I responded to the call."

"Who on earth is Cheryl Baremore?"

"I believe she is better known as Citrine, one name only, and has a popular blog that features her relationship with Eberschlag, A.K.A. Lucas Cross."

"Ah, her. What did they take?"

"Nothing, sir."

"How did she know she had an intruder?"

"She was at lunch, having an interview for *The Huffington Post*, when she received notification on her phone that someone was trying to unlock her iPad. It sent her a photo of the intruder. She called 911 and met me at her apartment. The intruder was gone before either of us arrived."

"Any sign of forced entry?"

"No, sir, but the lock could be easily slipped with a credit card."

Peter, who had returned to his paperwork, shook his head.

"What was disturbed?"

"Nothing, except the iPad."

"Fingerprints?"

"Wiped."

"At least you have the photo. Do you have a copy with you?"

"Yes, sir, though it won't do much good."

Peter swiveled around to look at the photo with Brent. The intruder's head was turning when the picture was snapped. It consisted of blurs of pink skin, grey hair, and patches that resembled camouflage. By some fluke, the only portion of the photo that could be identified was an ear that sprouted white hair.

"This is an older gent with an affection for camo," Brent said. "Does she have any idea who it is?"

"No, sir. Do you have any thoughts about this?"

"She probably has a stalker. I doubt if it's connected, but you never know. Thank you for calling this to my attention. If I need any more information, I'll let you know."

"Any time, sir."

Peter watched Cal navigate the treacherous path out of the bullpen. "Why do you let him do that?"

"Do what?"

"Call you sir all the time."

"If yon tadpole is under the mistaken impression that I outrank him, it would be rude of me to disabuse him. If he isn't, he's the only one here that has any manners." Brent stood up. "I feel like stretching my legs."

"I feel a bit stiff, myself."

Peter followed Brent outside to the edge of the parking lot, where Mount Storm Park verged onto the station. The lower end of the park was a nearly-impenetrable tangle of trees and undergrowth.

"Sometimes I wonder if Peter Max's cow liked to cavort in our parking lot for kicks late at night," Brent said.

"Sometimes you have too much time on your hands."

"It made me think. That cow is like the current situation. She became an international celebrity when she jumped a six-foot slaughterhouse fence and hid in those woods."

Peter smiled. "You think Eberschlag is back in the trees, mooning us right now? Guess that's as good a theory as any."

"That would be something, wouldn't it? Something puzzles me. The lady of your heart is working for the Lucas Cross machine, yet she is silent on the matter of his disappearance. How can that be?"

"Good sense on her part?"

"Such an innocent you are. Are you certain the Scooby Gang isn't up to something?"

"You noticed it too." Peter sighed.

"Furry ears and camo? It's not a positive ID, but it is troubling."

"Well, damn."

Peter found Lia stirring a pot in the kitchen, Chewy tied to her side. He bent down to pet the schnauzer. "Jail sucks, doesn't it, little guy?"

Viola, jealous, nosed in under his hand. "Okay, princess, you're the boss."

"Don't I get a hello pat?" Lia asked.

He stood up and gave her a smack on the rear.

"Hey! If you want to eat, be nice," she said.

"Smells good. What is it? Wait, let me guess. If we take out everything you can't eat, what's left?" He nuzzled her ear from behind. "Must be buffalo with kale and jicama."

"Smartie pants. It's beef stir fry on quinoa. Grab a plate. It's heavy on garlic and onions, so don't feed Viola under the table."

"Yes'm."

"So tell me," Peter asked, once the meal was well underway, "Do you hear anything from Sarah about Leroy?"

"Last I heard, the police in Austin were stymied. That was a week ago."

"You've been quiet about it. It seems a little strange, since you're close to his team."

"I think their stance is, the less said, the better."

Peter nodded into his quinoa. "What about your dog park friends? Aren't any of them curious about it?"

Lia set her chopsticks down. "What are you getting at, Peter?"

"A woman close to Leroy reported a break-in Friday." Peter watched Lia carefully. "Her iPad took a picture of the intruder. I can't imagine she has a gray-haired fanboy who wears camo. What's Terry up to these days?"

Lia shook her head. "Who was it? Was it Debby?"

"The lady has a right to privacy. Funny thing, she was meeting with a reporter for *The Huffington Post* when the break in happened. Brent called them, and they knew nothing about the reporter or the supposed story."

"Sounds like the journalist pumped up their prospects to get the interview."

"Or maybe it was a ruse to get her out of her apartment. If I ask the woman in question, will she tell me the interviewer was a tall, skinny red-head with a Cleopatra haircut?"

"Do you think Bailey was in on it?" Lia asked.

"Did you know about this?" Peter asked.

"They know you don't want me taking risks. It would be like Bailey and Terry to leave me out of the loop if they were doing something you wouldn't like. What do you call it? Deniability?"

Peter looked at her steadily.

"Peter, is this some kind of interrogation? If you want to know what happened, ask Terry. Or have Brent ask Terry. It's his case, isn't it?"

She knows more than she's saying, but saying so won't help anything.

"Babe, this is serious stuff. Nobody knows what's really going on, so anything can happen. The only thing we know is we aren't dealing with professional kidnappers, and that's a problem."

"How do you know they aren't pro?"

"Pros don't wait weeks to make a ransom demand."

"Oh."

"The Eberschlags did receive a ransom demand, but it was opportunistic punks. They had no clue where Leroy was."

"When was this? It wasn't in the news."

"For once, we kept everything quiet. The Eberschlags aren't talking about it. They were about to lose 50 thousand dollars when Cynth traced the email back to Elmwood Branch Library, where Debby Carrico works."

Lia gaped. "You don't think she had anything to do with it, do you?"

"No, it was teenagers at the library who overheard her talking about Leroy and thought they could pull a fast one."

"How did you catch them?"

"Debby remembered the conversation taking place after school was out, a few days before and around the same time as the email was sent. We pulled all the regular kids over twelve into the conference room and put the fear of God into them. Kids that age can't keep their mouths shut. We figured half the kids in that room knew about it. It didn't take long for a couple of them to crack.

"Thing is, a couple of the kids involved had access to guns. Kids with guns are much more dangerous than a pro with a gun."

"What's going to happen to them?"

"That's up to the courts. But this case is pulling in more nuts than a pecan convention. We get a dozen bogus sightings a day, and technically, it's not our case."

"I bet Brent loves that."

"He's gotten philosophical about it."

"Peter, do you know for sure it's Terry? Will he be arrested?"

Peter shrugged. "Not my case. Let's pretend we didn't have this conversation and get back to our regularly scheduled programming. Then I can ask if you had dessert in mind."

"I thought you were bringing dessert."

"Babe, I *am* dessert."

"Babe is a pig."

"I certainly hope so."

Chapter 9

Tuesday, June 28

"Egad," Terry said. "Do I need to leave the country?" He petted Jackson's head reassuringly. "Don't worry, old boy. If I go, I'll smuggle you and Napa out with me."

Lia surveyed the dog park parking lot. *No strange cars. If Brent was coming, he'd already be here.*

"I think Bailey saved you. I bet the photo is blurry."

"How do you know?" Bailey asked.

"I think Peter was fishing last night, to see what I knew. He deliberately only told me so much to see if I would fill in the blanks. If they could identify Terry from the photo, they would have gone to Terry. Peter would have shown me the photo. The photo is worthless, so he tells me they have it to see if I freak. They may do the same to either of you."

"If the photo is so bad, why do they think it's Terry?" Bailey asked.

"Peter said he didn't think the woman in question had a fanboy with gray hair and camo, then he asked what Terry was up to."

"He has a point," Terry said.

"If you plan to surrender, leave me out of it," Bailey said.

"Peter suggested they might ask 'the woman in question' to describe her interviewer. He seems to think she's tall and has red hair."

"At least he got that wrong," Bailey said.

"I forgot my Groucho Marx glasses. If they do ask her, I'm screwed."

Terry's face crumpled in concern. "I am duly chastised. How do we weather the storm?"

"Hold tight. I think Peter meant me to let you know that they know because they want us to squirm. I'm hoping this goes away. Whatever you do, do not mention Citrine. We know nothing about Citrine. Citrine does not exist. We don't even know it's a rock."

"I will essay to be more careful in the future," Terry said.

"Terry, there is no future. I'm out. I just had the most uncomfortable night of my life. I'm not putting my relationship with Peter at risk. No more Sherlock for me."

"What do you think?" Brent asked. He and Peter stood in the station parking lot at the start of shift. With the laughingly-named bullpen so crowded, this was the only place they could get a private word.

Peter took a slug of his morning Pepsi. "I think I hate sparring with Lia. She never gave anything away, but she spent too much time thinking. She was slow off the mark for critical questions and sometimes her responses didn't answer my questions. I hate when people do that. It's a sure sign they're hiding something."

"Maybe she was just worried about her friends. You didn't push her?"

"No, I didn't push her. I don't want my personal life to die an ugly death before this case ends. What do you plan to do?"

"I haven't decided. If it was Lia's friend, then it has nothing to do with Eberschlag, and pursuing it is a waste of time when I could be chasing down reports that he was eating a banana split at Putz's. If it was somebody else, we have no leads. But if you want to put a scare into the Scooby Gang, we can work something out."

"I like this hanging over their heads like the Sword of Damocles. I think the threat is more terrifying than the reality," Peter said. "And if nature takes its course, it will wind up coming out without bringing out the rubber hoses."

"Damocles? Pretty fancy for a boy from Kentucky." Brent's head jerked sideways at the sound of a car approaching. He was not an expert by any means, but he recognized the growl of that particular Ford Mustang. It belonged to Cynth, a goddess among women. "Oh, my heart," he sighed and watched out of the corner of his eye as she left her car.

Cynth downplayed her gorgeous figure by wearing her regulation polos two sizes too big. Fresh scrubbed skin and a no-nonsense braid were meant to keep her fellow officers at bay. It never worked.

Peter shook his head. "She hates you, you know."

"No she doesn't. She wants me so much she can't stand it, and only hates me by association with the passion she tries to deny."

"Uh-huh. ... Hey Cynth," Peter called.

"Hey yourself." Cynth looked down her nose at Brent, a neat trick because she was four inches shorter.

"Hey beautiful," Brent said.

"Peter, was someone speaking?"

He grinned. "Just the wind. Lia said to invite you to the Northside Parade. You want to see the neighborhood weirdos make idiots of themselves in a misguided expression of community spirit?"

"Sounds like fun. Who else will be there?"

"Just me, two dogs, and the wind. Think you can stand a little wind?"

"As long as you stay between me and the wind, I think I can handle it."

"Great. We've been given special dispensation to hang out on the library lawn. You might as well park here and take the bus up Hamilton Avenue. Just get there before 11:30 and bring water. There's a cookout afterwards."

"We'll see how it goes. I've got to get inside." Cynth continued on to the station, her wheat-colored braid swinging in counterpoint to her hips.

Peter watched Brent watching her. "She knows you're looking."

"She's crazy about me," Brent said.

Peter nodded his head. "I can see that."

Chapter 10

Saturday, July 2

Sarah, Alice, Carol, and Cecilie were inspecting the giant Browning Buckmark pistol as if it were a prize weimaraner at the Westminster dog show when Lia arrived at the garage. She stood in the doorway for a moment, judging their mood. Chewy, who had finally succumbed to his limitations, sat at her heel. Sarah looked up. Caught, Lia smiled and walked in.

"What do you think?" she asked.

"It's fabulous," Sarah said.

Alice lowered her glasses and tilted her head. "Much sexier than a Walther PPK."

Cecilie squinted through her wire rims. "I wish we didn't have to toss it in the dump."

"I would have nightmares about children climbing on it," Alice said. "And Jerry needs his trailer back."

"We'll want something different for next year. We have to stay competitive," Sarah said. "Think you can top this, Lia?"

Lia's immediate instinct was to widen her eyes, like a woodland creature trapped in headlights. *Next year? Am*

I supposed to pull this off again? "I, uh, guess we have time to think about it. Has Jerry installed the smoke machine yet?"

"Tomorrow afternoon," Sarah said. "We'll hang the banners and have a dress rehearsal. Then we'll hang the person who suggested we wear catsuits. Who was that anyway?"

"If you don't remember, the guilty party won't confess," Alice said.

"That was me," Carol said, leaning on a cane. "Five middle-aged women in spandex will be mild compared to other floats."

Chewy sniffed Carol's clunky support boot.

"Are you up for standing on a float with your ankle still healing?" Lia asked.

"I'm ready for a lighter brace, and I'll hang onto the gun when I need support," Carol said.

"I don't think any of us are in the right frame of mind to do this, with Leroy still missing," Alice said.

"We don't fight it. We use it. Go dark," Sarah said. "Like Tonya Harding in her Olympic bid after her ex-husband hired a thug to smash Nancy Kerrigan's knee."

"She imploded after that and was banned from skating. Do you want us to wind up on the women's boxing circuit?" Cecilie said. "Because I really hate getting hit in the face."

"We have 48 hours to figure out how to avoid that. I had new banners made up that will help. Did you bring an invoice, Lia?" Sarah asked, her eyes on the envelope in Lia's hand.

Lia gave it to Sarah. "Let me know if you have any questions."

"Carol will cut you a check first thing next week."

"Thanks." Lia stood, chewing on her lip. Chewy, picking up on her nerves, whined.

Sarah raised an eyebrow.

"I need to let you know, I think we've done all we can to find Leroy. I'm so sorry we weren't successful."

"I know," Sarah said. "I've been wondering if there was anything for you to find."

Alice looked at Sarah over her black frame glasses for a hard moment. "You did your best," she said.

Lia shrugged and quirked her mouth before she turned to go. Chewy circled smartly and followed her out, glued to her heel.

Chapter 11

Monday, July 4

Peter pulled his Explorer up to the U-Haul store next to the bedlam that was the parking lot of the Greater Bethlehem Temple Apostolic Church. The church was housed in a former grocery store, or perhaps it had been a roller rink. For years it sat with bare concrete walls and no windows, giving no hint to its purpose. Lia had never seen anyone go in or out, but the church must have a large congregation to afford renovations. Recently, an attractive entry with a porte cochere was added and the exterior walls were redone in a lovely cream color.

The property had been drafted into service for the Fourth of July parade years ago due to one compelling feature: the parking lot was larger than a football field.

Peter leaned over to kiss Lia good-bye but was blocked by Chewy, who sat on her lap, wearing his teal and fuchsia tulle ruff with a mutinous expression. Peter gave the dog a wry look.

"Chewy!" Lia admonished. She set her squirming fur-child firmly on her other side and leaned in for a healthy smooch.

"I'd tell you to break a leg," Peter said, tapping the dent in her chin, "but that would make it hard to march. You have your water?"

"Yes, sir, I also have doggie tutus, the travel bowl for Chewy, emergency poop bags and a pocket full of treats. Don't be such a worry wart." Lia opened her door. Chewy leapt out and she followed with her hip pack of survival gear and a garbage bag stuffed with tulle. Honey stuck her head out the back window and gave Lia a wounded look from the back seat while Viola climbed between the seats to claim Peter and the shotgun seat.

Lia petted Honey's silky head while Chewy tugged on his leash. "Take care of my baby, Dourson."

"Take care of mine, Anderson. We'll be watching for you from the library steps."

The crowd of costumed people milling around the parking lot of the church resembled the cantina scene in the first *Star Wars* movie. Floats were parked at the upper end of the lot, with marching groups filling the rest of the space. The morphing cacophony of color—only some of which was red, white and blue—was enough to induce motion sickness.

Lia grabbed the first person she could find with a clipboard and golf shirt, pegging the woman as a volunteer organizer. The woman checked her list and directed Lia across the lot, away from the monstrous gun Lia created.

She spotted Terry first, due to his insistence that he wear camouflage, and joined the group at their assigned spot in the line of floats and vehicles that zigzagged across the asphalt.

Lia pulled a ruff out of her bag and handed it to Terry. "Green, tan, and brown for Jackson," she said, "so you'll match."

Terry sighed. "If he has to wear a ruff, at least it's a manly ruff."

"'Manly ruff' is an oxymoron," Steve snorted as he stooped to slip a red and orange tutu over Penny's head.

"What do you think?" Lia asked. "I thought the color would show well with her black fur."

She continued to hand costumes around. Sophie, Nick's mastiff, dazzled in pink and purple, while Chester and Fleece sported traditional red, white and blue. Bailey and Renee compared tutus for Kita and Dakini, and decided to switch, with Dakini wearing green hues accented with gold and Kita in blues from sapphire to midnight, touched with bronze. The humans, with the exception of Terry, wore khaki in order to make the dogs stand out more.

The interminable wait was made longer because they were forced to stand. Lia looked enviously at the Ladies Lawn Chair Brigade, a dozen women who performed dance routines using vintage aluminum folding chairs. They currently relaxed on their props, chatting. *Whoever came up with their concept knew what they were doing.*

"I don't know why we had to check in by tenthirty," Bonnie said. "Some of us aren't twenty anymore."

"I bet it takes an hour to work their way down the line to make sure everyone is in the right spot," Bailey said.

"Take Chester for a stroll," Renee suggested. "If you walk by the lawn chair ladies and wilt a bit, maybe one of them will feel guilty and offer you her seat. If you wait a minute, I'll go with you. Then you can lean on me and look frail."

Lia looked up at the pale, grey sky, wondering if it would rain. The Browning Buckmark loomed over the crowd, overshadowed only by a giant, upended plunger built by a local plumber. The parade would go on no matter what the weather. *At least we don't need the dog booties. With no sun, the pavement won't get hot enough to burn paws.*

"We might get a sprinkle or two," Jim said, reading her mind. "Nothing more."

"Balderdash," Terry said. "We're in for a frog strangler. I checked radar."

"I hope we don't get any thunder," Bailey said, tweaking Kita's tutu into a more attractive arrangement. "Kita doesn't like it. How long do you think the rain will last?"

"All afternoon. We'll be drenched by the time we pass The Comet," Terry opined. "That is, if they can get this show on the road. If not, we'll drown before we're out of the parking lot. Today's bar-b-ques are toast. Nobody wants soggy bratwurst."

"No rain," Jim insisted. "We'll be fine."

"If we don't get a downpour during the parade, I'll wear a Bill Clinton tee shirt every Saturday until Labor Day," Terry said. "Sure you don't want my spare pocket poncho?"

"Deal," Jim said. "Keep your poncho. You'll need it to catch the tears you'll be crying when you lose this bet."

"Jim, I wish you wouldn't bet," Bonnie said.

"Wait a minute," Bailey said. "What does Jim do if he loses?"

"I'll wear any tee shirt you choose every Saturday. Till Labor Day," Jim volunteered.

"Done. I'm going to stretch my legs. We've been standing here too long," Terry said, chortling to himself as he meandered into the crowd, Jackson trotting obediently after him.

"You know he's sneaking off to surf for the most offensive tee shirt he can find," Bailey said.

"I can't believe you made that bet," Steve said.

"He'll never let you forget it," Lia said. "And *you*—" she turned to Bailey. "Why did you have to say anything about Jim's side of the bet?"

Bailey shrugged. "Fair is fair. Besides, Jim—Ow!" She leaned over to rub her ankle, giving Jim a murderous look.

"Did you just kick Bailey?" Bonnie asked, dumbfounded.

"He did," Bailey said. "I don't know why. You were going to tell, anyway."

"Tell what?" Lia demanded.

Jim ducked his head, looking sheepish. "We set Terry up."

"I don't understand," Bonnie said.

"It was a sucker bet. The rain is going to miss us. My knee always hurts before it rains, and it feels fine. I've been waiting years for the right time to pull this on him."

"Oh. Well that's all right, then," Bonnie said.

Lia knelt down in the crowd and petted Chewy, who was trying to scratch his ruff off when he wasn't dancing back and forth in agitation. "Can you believe that, Little Man? Your Uncle Jim is being sneaky and underhanded. But at least you won't get wet."

Unused to the crush of people in bizarre costumes, the dogs remained by their owners, partly guarding, partly out of insecurity. Lia stood up and shifted from one foot to the other, anxious to get going.

"I just hope the dogs don't freak when the noise starts," she said.

"Relax." Bailey dismissed Lia's concern with a wave of one bird-like hand. "By now they're immune to tubas and drums."

"Twelve-ten," Jim said. "They're late."

"It's tradition," Jose said.

"The road is blocked off." Bailey nodded at the orange and white traffic barriers and the policemen re-routing traffic. It won't be long now. Bonnie and Renee are still hanging with the lawn chair ladies. I'll go get them."

Lia became aware of a murmur rising at the south entrance to the parking lot. It swept back towards them, growing in volume as it approached. All around her, people straightened up and made last minute checks while volunteers in golf shirts trotted down the line.

At some invisible signal, Oliver Kroner pulled a child's red wagon out onto Hamilton Avenue then turned south to wild cheers that rolled over the crowd with a sudden infusion of exuberance. The cheers carried from the parking lot to the residents camped along both sides of the road and would follow the wagon on the mile and a half procession to Hoffner Park.

Lia laughed and bounced up on her toes to see the wagon's passenger, this year's two year-old grand marshall, Quincy Kroner. Quincy was escorted by a garbage man who had appeared with him in a photograph that went viral in the spring, making Quincy Northside's most famous resident at the moment.

Quincy was followed by CAIN, the neighborhood food pantry, whose employees wheeled donation barrels painted like Campbell's Soup cans. The Mill Creek Yacht Club's members high-fived onlookers with canoe paddles while an old Woodie station wagon loaded with five canoes crawled along behind.

The front of the parade expanded like a caterpillar inching forward and extruded out onto the avenue as each group lined up in proper formation and exited the parking lot. All eyes were on the road, as this would be the only opportunity most of the marchers would have to see the parade in action. Music started haltingly, then gained confidence and volume as marchers found their rhythm.

Along with the usual fire trucks and vintage cars, high school bands blared while midriff-baring drill teams strutted and shook their booties. Snazzy convertibles carried politicians who queen-waved the crowd while their supporters ran along the curbs passing out candy and pamphlets. Such things were mandatory for community parades.

Northside was famous for being friendly, funky and outrageous. The parade was an excuse for residents to raid their attics to create the most outlandish displays they could conceive. Parade entries ran from the slapdash and outright lazy to wonders of architecture and artistry.

Chicken Lays an Egg dressed in vintage clothes topped with amazing headdresses that made *Hunger Games's* District One couture pale and tame in comparison. A body builder, oiled to maximum sheen in his speedo, strutted curbside, stopping frequently to pose. An old pickup towed a skateboard ramp painted with an enormous skull of a longhorn steer. Boarders launched off the truck, buzzed the crowd and ascended back up the ramp to do tricks. A sauntering procession of shirtless young men in kilts carried a banner that proclaimed "Free Willie."

Some of the floats were out of season, including a hearse topped with pumpkins and a float covered in cotton "snow," sporting Christmas trees while a man sang a soulful Jingle Bells into a PA system and elves waved to the crowd.

The parade oozed out of the parking lot and the line inched forward. Lia estimated it would take close to an hour before the Dog Stars made it to the street. *Hurry up and wait. Next year, I'll hire a double to stand in line for me. I'll sit across the street with the spectators instead.*

Chewy whined and squatted. Lia sighed and pulled out one of her emergency poop bags. She stepped out of line with Chewy's mess in hand, hoping to find a trash can near the church entry. Lia stepped beyond the edge of the crowd and a familiar figure popped into view.

Citrine was alone, leaning against the side of the building. *The one time and place where she won't stick out like an eskimo at a beach party. Dammit! She's coming over.* Lia kept her eyes averted in hope she was mistaken about Citrine's intentions. No such luck. Citrine intercepted her at the trash can.

"I never imagined seeing you here. Oh, look at the adorable ruff!" She stooped to pet Chewy, who had no standards and did not care who gave him attention. "Is he yours? You must be in the parade."

"Yeah, my friends and I are performing formations with our dogs."

Lia turned to rejoin her group. Citrine followed.

"What fun! I've never seen anything like that in the parade before. Hey, guess what, that guy who broke into my apartment left without taking anything. I guess having his picture taken scared him away. Freaky, huh?"

"That's lucky. Do the police know who he is?"

"They say they're still looking. I gave the landlord hell and he installed a deadbolt, so he won't get in again even if he comes back. By the way, I've been watching *The Huffington Post*, and I haven't seen your article yet. When is it coming out?"

Does she plan to follow me all the way to Hoffner Park? "I, uh, I've been having a hard time hooking up with Leroy's family. I'm hoping to talk to them after the parade." *Shit, shit, shit! I have to get rid of her before she sees Terry.* Lia looked wildly around the crowd, hoping a diversion would present itself. "Are you in the parade, too?"

"Me? Oh, no. I know a couple of the guys with MO-BI." Citrine pointed to a group of bare-chested bicycle nerds on Frankensteined bicycles and unicycles, some with seats six feet off the ground, riding in lazy circles around the ever-widening open space at the back of the lot. "I thought it would be fun to follow them down the hill."

Oh, great. That means she could notice Terry at any time. They were now twenty feet from the dog parkers, with Terry's signature camo in full view. *Dammit, desperate times, desperate measures.*

"Have you seen Leroy's aunt Debby? She's on the float with the giant gun. I think they're short a person for the float. You should go talk to her."

"Wow! Wouldn't that be fun," Citrine immediately veered off, then hesitated. "Keep me posted about the article, won't you?"

Lia watched until Citrine was fifty feet away, then tapped Terry on the shoulder. He whipped around.

"Wha—"

Lia whispered in his ear. "Citrine's here. You have to switch shirts with Steve and ditch your hat." She searched the group for Terry's roommate.

Steve made a disgusted face. "You want me to what? Wear his sweaty shirt? You've got to be kidding."

"If you don't, you may wind up without someone to split the rent with," Lia said.

"What's this about?" Steve asked.

"You didn't tell him?" Lia asked Terry.

"Er, no," Terry said. "I was trying to be discrete."

Meaning he felt like an idiot and was hoping no one would find out.

"You can explain later." She turned back to Steve. "Just trust me on this."

A volunteer trotted up, clipboard in hand. She looked the group up and down. "Mount Airy Dog Stars? Everybody ready? Get into formation. Make sure your rows are spaced to take up at least ten feet across. Next up is the Lucas Cross float, then we have La Boiteaux Woods, and then you and your dogs."

Message delivered, she moved on to corral the stylists from Taylor Jameson Hair Design, who were dressed in flowing white gowns with ferns and flowers twined in their hair as if they'd just walked off the set of *A Midsummer's Night Dream.*

The line halted while volunteers guided the Browning Buckmark out onto Hamilton Avenue. Lia took a moment to feel dizzy. She hadn't realized how monumental it would appear, looming over the road, and how tiny Sarah's crew would look standing next to it on the flatbed. *It's like the Queen Mary on her maiden voyage.*

"It brings tears to your eyes, does it not?" Terry said from the second row. Lia felt the cheer well up and rip out of her throat. She waved wildly.

Stealthy spy music played from a speaker on top of Jerry's truck. Smoke wisped out of the gun barrel while Fiber and Snark, dressed in scavenged versions of Koi's signature catsuit, took stealthy poses around the grip of the giant Browning.

Alice placed one hand on her hip and reached up to stroke the bottom of the gun's trigger guard in a pose to make any game show hostess proud. Carol, sporting a new, slimmer leg brace, took a haughty pose and snapped a short whip. Debby fired a few experimental shots with a water pistol upon the onlookers, causing delighted children to run into the street to catch the spray and beg to be "shot." Cecilie joined Debby in firing on the children.

Where's Sarah? Lia counted again, but saw no sign of her. *Maybe she has something special planned. I bet she'll emerge from the crowd as an enemy agent.*

La Boiteux Woods Nature Center followed with an adorable hive of children dressed as bees in yellow tee shirts and flapping enormous poster board wings. They kept trying to move into range for Debby's water gun while happily buzzing around.

Lia's heart swelled with anticipation as she stood at the edge of the road, waiting for their cue. The volunteer at the curb blew two short blasts on her whistle. Lia looked over at Nick, Renee, and Steve. Renee nodded. The third blast came and the Mount Airy Dog Stars stepped forward in unison, smiles plastered to their faces as they waved to the cheering crowd, every dog at heel.

Lia took time to appreciate Renee's influence with the parade committee. Placed between the Nature Center Bees and Taylor Jaimeson's Grecian Nymphs, there was little to disturb the dogs, though Chewy looked longingly at the nature center bees, their flight pattern resembling dog park chases. Still, the incarceration of the last month had his duty firmly imprinted on his doggy soul and he stayed at Lia's heel.

"I'm proud of you, Little Man," Lia said as they marched.

Peter kept Honey and Viola close while he surveyed the crowd gathering on the library lawn. The century-old, red brick building was a classic Carnegie library, one of their standard designs. "What do you think about sitting under the tree?" he asked Brent, who was carrying three camp chairs, their straps slung over his shoulder.

"I think I don't care, as long as I get to put these chairs down."

Chuck, Sarah's assistant librarian, was a tall and substantial young man with a long ponytail and impressive wizard's beard. He stood on the walkway in front of the building, swinging his arm back and forth in the air to catch their attention.

"C'mon up here," he yelled.

They walked up the rise to meet Chuck, who bent down to pet the dogs.

"You have plastic bags in case they hear the call of nature?"

Peter pulled the end of a grocery bag out of his pocket to show Chuck, who responded with a fist bump.

"My man. View's better from here. It's best from the top of the steps, but Diane and Barbara called dibs on those spots in February. They have seniority and got to pick first. You can also sit on the steps, but you need serious cushioning to stand the concrete for two hours."

"The shade is down by the bus stop," Peter pointed out.

"Feel free, but you'll get crushed," Chuck said.

"We have hats," Brent said. "I think we can handle a little sun."

"Good choice. I'm your unofficial host." He put his hand in his pocket, and withdrew a keyring. "I have keys to the back door. If you find yourself in need of the facilities, let me know. I'll be sitting over there." Chuck pointed to an empty camp chair next to a cooler.

They set up the chairs. Peter sat in the middle. Viola, who liked to lurk in dark, den-like spaces, crawled underneath. Honey sat in front of Peter, grinning.

"Why do you get to sit in the middle?" Brent asked. "I want to sit in the middle."

"You just want to sit next to Cynth. She made me promise that she would not have to sit next to you. What did you ever do to her, anyway?"

"Well, we're here," Brent said, changing the subject. "What do we do now?"

"Let's see," Peter said. "It's not quite eleven-twenty. The parade starts in 40 minutes, then it will take another hour to get here and will last at least an hour after that."

"We have to wait an hour and forty minutes before this gala event gets off the ground?" Brent asked, incredulous. "What is it about Cincinnati, that the locals enjoy crowding into public spaces where nothing is happening?"

"You can people watch. Take pictures."

"True," Brent said, observing the stream of people passing by. He eyed a man in a clown outfit carrying a boa constrictor. "I imagine some of these folks are more outlandish than the parade. And speaking of outlandish …"

Cynth arrived, wearing a red, white, blue and gold tutu and a skin tight tank over red high-top sneakers. Her hair piled on top of her head, held there with a wreath made of tulle scraps. Peter could not tell if the low whining noises he heard came from Honey or Brent. He kicked Brent's ankle as Cynth bent over to set down a small cooler, exposing tiny blue shorts covered with white stars.

"I thought I would get in the spirit of things," she said as she plopped down next to Peter.

Peter could only nod.

Lia watched Citrine trail the Savage Gun float down the hill to Millionaire's Corner, occasionally disappearing, presumably to watch the MOBI guys. She'd shown no interest in the Dog Stars. Terry was safe as long as he didn't run into her when the parade dispersed.

The Dog Stars were performing their weave when Lia thought she saw something in the gun barrel of the Savage Gun float. Smoke billowed out, obscuring her vision so that the thing was reduced to a dark blotch. Distracted, she hesitated long enough for Jim and Fleece to bump into her from behind. Chewy protested with a yelp.

"Pay attention," Jim said.

"Sorry," She moved ahead and forgot about the anomaly, concentrating on leading Chewy through the routine correctly.

They continued down Hamilton Avenue, passing a series of houses that sat up on a rise, giving everyone in the yards a great view. One lawn hosted a party of colorfully draped people playing every manner of percussive instruments. Paul Ravenscraft, local massage therapist, world musician, and non-denominational minister, stopped drumming on his djembe to give her a wave.

Heeling in formation gave Lia a chance to look at the gun barrel again. She could see more of the thing now, dangling a foot below the barrel, and joined by a second something, both swaying in unison. A window appeared in the smoke, closing in again before Lia could get more than an impression.

The things resembled forearms.

Lia stared at the smoke, willing it to part again. It did not oblige her before the next stop, when she was forced to focus on the complicated routine. Chewy was tired and balked at performing.

She slipped a liver treat out of her hip pack and held it close to his nose to lure him along. The stratagem worked, though she had to cage the treat in her fingers so he could not take it from her, and his performance was marred by periodic lunges of his head.

When Lia had a chance to look up again, she could have sworn that the gun barrel was a few inches lower. Two arms now extended fully from the gun barrel, dangling limply in a tangle of long hair from what could only be Sarah's head—who else but Sarah had that hair?—bobbing fluidly with the movement of the float as smoke continued to twine around her.

Lia snorted a laugh. The Northside parade was famous for outrageous floats. *Looks like Sarah decided to outdo everybody.* The knitting ladies in their catsuits amped up their voguing around the float as more people pointed, laughing and snapping pictures.

Any minute now, Sarah will lift her head up and wave. Lia mentally shook her head and tried to remember what Jose used to anchor the barrel onto the gun's grip. *I hope it can support Sarah's weight.*

The Dog Stars spread out at their next stop for their square dancing routine.

A cracking sound came out of nowhere.

Lia jerked her head up, scanning the parade and sidewalks for the source. She saw people looking around, as clueless as she was.

"What was that? a gunshot?" Bailey asked as she do-si-doed with Lia.

"Wrong noise," Lia yelled after her, returning to her place next to Jose.

Chewy stayed by Lia's side while she and Jose switched partners with Jim and Bonnie. Next, all the women stood while the men wove around them. Terry started on his pass. Chewy began whining, head bumping

Lia's shin. She stooped unobtrusively and gave his head a little pat.

"You're doing fine, Little Man. The parade will be over before long."

Chewy stood up and howled. The other dogs abandoned the routine and joined him, straining their leashes towards the front of the parade.

Lia could barely hear the loud groaning noise over the dogs. She looked ahead in time to see the barrel of the giant gun tilting down, slowly at first. She stared in horror as it picked up speed, slamming against the end of the trailer and summersaulting Sarah like a rag-doll into a heap on the road.

The gun barrel broke free of its insufficient mooring and bounced end over end on the pavement, barely missing Sarah's motionless form. It rebounded, looming over spectators who scrambled and stumbled out of their chairs as it came crashing down. Lia caught sight of Citrine shrieking as a woman twice her size mowed her down.

Peter leapt out of his chair at the first scream, Cynth and Brent were close behind. Cynth stuffed Viola and Honey's leashes in Peter's hand while the dogs stared at him in accusation for abandoning them. Together they shoved through crowds to reach the disturbance, whatever it was.

Spectators were torn between staying in their chairs to keep their prime seats or surging up Hamilton Avenue to see what happened. Either way, they created an obstacle.

Brent was the first to break out of the crowd and directly in the path of the parade. The trio dodged around the cycle geeks and cut through a girls' dance team. Their path cleared after that as they ran alongside a column of antique cars. The decapitated Browning loomed ahead.

Peter urged the dogs to run faster. *Oh, God, I hope it's not Lia.*

The honeybees ran screaming from the careening gun barrel and its macabre load. Lia darted through the evacuating children to get to Sarah's side, still holding Chewy's leash. Bailey and Kita were behind her with the rest of her team.

"Oh my God, oh my God! I thought it was a joke! I thought she was pretending to be dead!" Lia dropped onto her knees.

Sarah lay on her side, head twisted and limbs flung wide in a grotesque imitation of 60's freestyle dancing. Hundreds of onlookers pressed in, forming a circle enclosing Lia with Bailey, Sarah and the dogs. Kita and Chewy whined.

The color of Sarah's skin caught Lia's attention. It was was pink, not white. She pressed two fingers to Sarah's throat, above a ring of purpling bruises. She felt nothing and started to panic. *Calm down. Try another spot.* She slid her fingers up under Sarah's jaw. Still nothing. She slid her fingers back an inch. Sarah's pulse was faint, but there.

"Thank God," Lia said. "She's alive."

Bailey turned around, yelling to the crowd, "We need a doctor or a medic! Do we have a doctor or EMT?"

With the temperature in the 90s and the humidity almost as high, it was harder to tell if Sarah was breathing. Lia grabbed a wisp of Sarah's hair and held it under her nose. The hair fluttered.

Bailey repeated her plea for help.

A burly young man dressed in a paisley caftan pushed through the crowd, followed by a smaller man and a woman. By their clothing, Lia guessed they had been at the drumming party with Paul.

The trio snapped into action, the smaller man feeling Sarah's limbs for broken bones while the woman took her vitals and the burly man checked her pupils. Lia and Bailey stood back to let them work.

Debby forced a path through, followed by the rest of Fiber and Snark.

"What happened?" Debby demanded.

Sirens split the air. The crowd opened up on one side to let the ambulance through. Paisley caftan machine gunned the vital information to the ambulance crew while they eased Sarah onto a backboard and loaded her into the ambulance.

With the ambulance gone, the crowd melted back to the sidewalks, leaving Lia and Bailey to face a hysterical knitting club and several police officers. The dog park gang stood by the side of the road, waiting for Lia and Bailey. Jerry stood guard over the broken float, chasing away spectators who wanted souvenirs.

Hamilton Avenue was clear for several blocks ahead, the front half of the parade having moved on, though the MOBI cyclists and a couple of random roller bladers swooped back around, not wanting to miss any of the action.

Police officers herded spectators to the side of the road and led Lia, Bailey, and Fiber and Snark behind the float, now parked at the curb. The rest of the Dog Stars joined them while two more officers directed the parade past the scene. Lia thought she recognized Cal Hinkle by his straw-colored hair.

Rubbernecking marchers moved silently by as if in paying respect to the accident. They resumed their honking, blaring, gyrating cacophony once they were beyond the catastrophe. It was odd, this black hole puncturing the center of the parade route, sucking in all celebration within its reach.

While many spectators stayed to observe the proceedings, most folded their chairs and left, many of those carrying a chair in one hand while leading a tearful child with the other.

Lia sat on the end of the trailer, watching as park employees led the honeybees back into the parade, resuming their march. At a time when each of those children desperately needed comfort, they had nowhere to go but forward. Solace was more than a half-mile away at the end of the parade route, where their parents waited. They walked huddled together for safety, no longer the exuberant melee of before. The bees had lost their buzz.

How much do they understand? How long will they have bad dreams?

Lia absorbed sound and color but comprehended little. She had always been responsive in an emergency—it was afterwards she fell apart. Now that fearful place deep inside herself did its hysterical best to lure Lia into the fetal position. *Just breathe. That's what Asia says. Just breathe.* She became aware of Chewy whining.

"Sorry, Little Man." She picked him up and held him in her lap, rubbing her cheek against the fur on top of his head.

"What did you see, Lia?" Debby had her arm now and pulled her attention away from the children. "All we knew was the top of the gun fell over and Sarah came out. No one knows why she was up there."

Alice opened her mouth, but stayed silent when one of the officers shook his head.

"Ladies, please keep to yourselves. We need everyone's memories intact and uncontaminated," the officer said. "We'll be taking your statements separately. A couple of detectives will be here in a few minutes to talk to you."

As he spoke, Lia spotted Peter, Brent, and Cynth cutting in front of a cherry-red Model T Ford and aiming for their conclave. Peter led Viola and Honey on their leashes. The Model T a-OOGaed in protest and Viola assumed a combative stance, barking maniacally while Honey strained towards Lia. Lia groaned. *Now it's all going to come out.*

"What's the matter, Lia?" Steve asked. "You're looking sick."

"I kind of am," she replied.

"Peter," Lia said as he trotted up. She held out her free hand to take Honey and Viola's leashes. Honey jumped up on the trailer and curled at her side. Viola, anticipating separation from Peter, sulked.

He gave her a wry look. "This isn't what I meant when I said to take care of yourself, Babe."

Lia said nothing.

Peter gave her a searching look.

"All right," Brent said, "word is we have a nearly dead body by the name of Sarah Schellenger, who fell out of this float when it came apart." He pointed at the shambles. "In front of you and a bunch of dogs and some traumatized kids just out of diapers. I don't think the kids or dogs will be much help, so it's up to you all to tell us what happened. Is this your entire group, Lia?"

Lia glanced around and did a quick head count. "Yes, this is everybody."

"Okay, who was watching the float when it fell apart?"

Steve, Jim and Lia raised their hands.

Brent continued, "Who was watching it during the parade?"

Everyone raised their hands.

"Brent," Lia interrupted, "you should grab Citrine. She followed the float all the way down the hill, and she was taking pictures."

"Citrine? Leroy's supposed girlfriend? Where is she?" He craned his neck around, searching the crowd. For once, Citrine's alarming orange hair was lost in the outrageously attired crowd.

"Last I saw, she was talking to one of the off duty EMTs, a guy in a purple caftan. I think she may have been hurt in the crush."

Brent sighed. "I'll get Hinkle on it."

It's a hell of a statement, dropping a dead body in the middle of a parade. Attention seeking or poor planning? I bet not one of the thousands of people who saw the float saw anything helpful.

Peter surveyed the remains of the giant gun and wished he could climb up to see if the structure had been tampered with. *Can't though, with the attention this case will have, Roller will have my ass if I don't leave it for the CSIs. Well, what's there won't disappear. Not like memories. Witnesses first.*

The ladies of Fiber and Snark drooped in the heat, despite having taken advantage of the float's towering presence to wait in the shade. *Full length, black cat suits, in this heat. I'm surprised none of them have fainted.*

"Ladies," he said, nodding his head in greeting. "I think it's going to take a while to get your statements. What if we get you out of this heat?"

The women nodded in unison.

Brent raised his eyebrows. "Where do you propose we go? We don't have room for 12 civilians at the station."

"Chuck has keys to the library so the employees could sneak in the back to use the bathroom. I bet he's public spirited enough to let us use the building to take statements."

"Okay folks! We'd like to use the library to take your statements. I believe you'll be more comfortable there. Does anyone have Chuck's phone number so we can work out the details?"

"What about the dogs?" Debby asked.

"If we use the elevator and go down to the activity room, it should be okay," Alice said. That's a vinyl floor. Any messes will be easy to clean up."

"I'll call Chuck," Debby said.

"Wait a minute. I'm not leaving my truck and trailer behind," Jerry insisted, his face turning red. "I've got too much money tied up in them."

Peter made a quick mental calculation of the man's proprietary interest in the well-being of his truck against Peter's own need for cooperation. "We've got an officer here to protect your truck and trailer until the crime scene folks can take possession of them—"

Jerry squawked, "Take my truck? I need that truck for my business. You can't take my truck!"

Peter knew there was no way to rescue the situation, but he did his best. "Where was the truck last night?"

"In front my house."

"And the float?"

"Three miles away, at my garage. You taking my garage, too?"

Peter decided he was not going to be the one to tell Jerry Carrico that likely, his garage would be out of commission for at least half a day while it was searched. "Since the truck wasn't with the float until right before the parade, it's possible crime scene can release it to you within 24 hours. I'll tell them to process it first, so we can eliminate it."

"Thank you," Jerry grumbled.

Peter sent a text Cynth, who was talking to a group of spectators further up the block. She gave Peter a wave, then came over to join them. Jerry's eyes lit up at the multi-colored tulle, vision, then jerked his head around to see if Debby was watching. *Yes, Jerry, you have a wife.*

"Mr. Carrico, this is Detective McFadden. She'll take your statement here so you won't have to leave your vehicle."

"Happy to," Cynth said, smiling in her deceptively sweet way. "Mr. Carrico, lets see if we can borrow some lawn chairs while we take care of this." Jerry followed her like a puppy, over to the curb.

Peter turned back to the group. "Who's ready for a short hike?"

"So the float was locked in Jerry's garage," Terry mused as he selected jalapeno peppers and muenster cheese from the loaded buffet in Jim's yard and layered them on his hamburger. "I'm not convinced this is Leroy's doing. Could it be a love triangle gone wrong? Was the lithe and lovely librarian cavorting with the earthy grease monkey after hours? Caught in flagrante delicto by the wronged wife?"

"Doubtful," Lia said, forking up a bite of bunless burger off her paper plate. She looked down at a sea of salivating muzzles and cut off pieces to share. "Not that Debby wouldn't do it. I don't think Jerry is Sarah's type. And Debby's not strong enough to shove Sarah inside the float."

"Ah, but the cheating husband would assist his wife, as that would be the only way to keep his own ass out of a sling," Terry said.

"Why wouldn't Jerry just stop Debby from strangling her?" Bailey asked.

Nick guffawed. "Interfering in a cat fight is dangerous. Would you jump into a cat fight, Jim?"

"Not me," Jim said, shuddering.

"No wise man would," Steve said.

"I saw them talking before the parade," Bailey said, taking a bite of pickle. "They didn't look like they knew there was a body on board, dead of otherwise. And neither of them was any more freaked out than anyone else after Sarah appeared."

"If I was hiding a body and it fell out in front of a thousand people, I wouldn't be able to keep my cool. I sure wouldn't be able to put on a good act of being shocked. I'd just look guilty as hell," Steve said.

"The butler did it," Jim said, handing a loaded plate to Bonnie before starting one for himself.

Terry waved him off. "Bah! It's always the spouse. If Debby didn't do it, Duane did."

"Bad back," Lia said, her eyes glued to her plate. *Patience, Anderson. These are your friends.* "They're all middle-aged and feeling it. Duane's scheduled for surgery. If he picked Sarah up, he'd be in the hospital before he could make it two feet."

"Why don't you think it was Leroy, Terry?" Bonnie asked. "Jim told me about your investigations. Seems to me he's the logical suspect."

"Nobody can find Leroy," Terry said. "We can find everyone else."

"Funny thing," Jose said. "I can't believe the float lasted a mile, carrying a load like that."

"The angle of the gun barrel kept her weight back in the tube while they were coming down the hill," Jim explained. "Once the ground leveled, her weight shifted, and the barrel acted like a lever."

"Once an engineer, always and engineer," Bailey said. "If Leroy and Duane and Jerry didn't do it, who did? And why?"

"Perhaps she ran afoul of Jerry's meth-addled mechanic emerging from his secret drug lab," Terry bobbed his eyes suggestively.

"Jerry doesn't have a drug-addled meth-head working for him," Steve said.

"And how do you know?" Terry said.

"Because he'd be an idiot if he did. And even a meth-head knows better than to cook drugs near all those flamable chemicals," Steve said.

"There's no place for a drug lab." Lia said patiently. "The garage is one huge empty room, like a concrete airplane hanger. You might as well say the rest of Sarah's knitting club ganged up on her and did it," Lia said.

"By George, you've nailed it!" Terry said.

Jim shook his head. Steve rolled his eyes.

"Terry, I wish you'd stop joking about this," Lia said. "Sarah is my friend, and I don't know if she's ever going to wake up. Excuse me."

Lia headed for the house, followed by a train of dogs. She sat on the back steps. Honey, as always, sensed her mood and leaned on her. Chewy eyed her hopefully for more burger. No longer hungry, she picked pieces of burger off her plate and lobbed them to the dogs.

Idiots. They act like this is a game.

Bonnie sat down next to Lia and put a hand on her knee. "You have every right to be upset, seeing that happen to your friend. I know they sound insensitive, but I think it might be their way of handling it."

"Like cop humor?"

"Something like that."

"I just want to sit here for a while. I'll rejoin the group in a bit."

Bonnie departed, leaving Lia to the ministrations of the dogs. Lia sat, thinking about nothing and focused on her breathing until her stomach settled. She realized she was hungry and headed back to the table and human society.

"One thing's for sure," Terry said. "If Sarah, wakes up, she'll be able to identify him. He has to finish the job."

Lia shut her eyes and considered fleeing for the steps again. She and Bailey looked at each other. Bailey winked.

"Oh? And are you planning to set a trap?" Steve asked.

"Yeah," Jose said. "I seen that in movies. That would be awesome. Hide under the sheets with a gun, and when the killer comes, POW!"

"You get the hospital to let you in Sarah's room with a gun, and I'll use my feminine wiles to lure her police guard away so the killer will think the coast is clear," Bailey offered.

"What hospital is going to let you in her room with a gun? You could be the killer, pretending to set a trap for the killer," Jim said.

"You're right," Bailey said. "I'll have to offer the officer a quickie in the supply closet to keep him away long enough for Terry to sneak in and the killer to show up. Do you think it will be Officer Brainard, Lia? I could sure keep him busy."

"This is stupid," Jim said. The killer is going to see a big, fat lump under the sheets and know someone is hiding there."

"True," Terry said, scratching the stubble on his chin. "Lia, you'll have to do it. You're small enough."

"Me? Don't drag me into this."

"You at least have to go to the hospital, and see who's keeping vigil," Terry urged.

"I will not intrude on her friends and family."

"You're her friend. You have a plausible reason for showing up," Terry said. "We can chip in for flowers. If I show up, they might find it strange. Still, if I profess to offer my best wishes to a member of Lucas Cross' entourage as a fan of the Colt Savage novels, it might fly."

"I'll go," Lia said. "But only because I want to check on her. And only if you promise to stay away. I'll go tomorrow. They might know something then."

"And by then you will have charmed vital information from the delectable Detective Dourson," Terry said.

"Lia, you don't have to do this if you don't want to," Steve said. "I can just strangle Terry in his sleep tonight."

Long after the bar-b-que leftovers were wrapped, just as the opening salvos of the annual Armageddon of neighborhood fireworks were launching into the clammy evening air, Peter stepped into Lia's air conditioning and said a silent prayer of gratitude for the end of a long, hot, sticky day. He plopped wearily onto Lia's colorful Mission style couch, leaning his head back to rest on the top of the cushion and shut his eyes.

Viola, who was under the sofa with Chewy to get away from the fireworks, nosed out from her hidey hole and climbed up next to him, snuggling tightly for protection. She nudged her muzzle under Peter's hand and he petted her without thinking. Honey, an old hand with fireworks, headed into the kitchen. Peter heard the refrigerator door open and shut.

"Bless you, wonderful woman," he said.

Lia returned, handing him a beer. "Scoot onto the floor. I'll rub your shoulders."

Peter thought this was a fine idea but wisely curbed the ready remark about how she could do this daily if they got married.

"Scooted." Viola jumped down and crawled into his lap as a trio of rockets burst, flashing fuchsia, green and gold outside the windows.

"Take off your shirt."

"Demanding, aren't you?" He sat forward to comply and Lia slipped onto the sofa behind him.

"I can always keep my thumbs to myself."

"Heaven forbid. Demand away, Babe."

He felt her warm breath on his ear.

"Babe," she said sweetly, digging her thumbs into twin pressure points/sore spots, "is a pig."

"Ow. I get your point."

He took a pull from the chilled bottle as she gripped his trapezius muscles and pressed her thumbs into the tissue. The tension of the day melted away. The air conditioning chilled the sweat on his body while her circling thumbs worked their way up his vertebrae one by one, then dug into the base of his skull.

Marry Me. The words almost slipped out. *Damn Dourson, a little beer, and you lose your filters. You must love sleeping on that couch.*

He inhaled deeply, sighed.

"Rough day?" Lia asked.

Peter rolled his head, felt the give in his muscles.

"I don't know what to think about this one. It's the strangest case I've ever worked."

"How so?" Her thumbs were now stroking under his shoulder blades.

"We've got a corpse that's not dead, and no obvious motives or suspects. Husband out of town for a gig, that's confirmed."

"How is Sarah?"

"She's in a coma, probably as a result of asphyxiation, complicated by head injury from her fall. Someone strangled her, then hid the body in that float. Since she wasn't dead, we don't have lividity to tell us what position she was in when they strangled her. Brent and I went to the garage. We didn't find any signs of a struggle, so we can't say for sure if she was attacked at the garage or if she was taken there after the attack.

"The bruises the EMT described suggest she was strangled with a rope or noose, but there's also a very odd mark on her neck, and we won't know what that is until we can photograph it. We'll know more tomorrow after the crime scene folks have a chance to look for trace evidence on her clothes.

If there was any trace evidence on her body, chances are it was lost when she was prepped for surgery. She was rushed into surgery, so no one had a chance to examine her for defensive wounds, but one of the EMTs attending her said her hands and arms weren't injured."

"Why do you think that is?""

Lia's hands stilled. She leaned her forehead onto his shoulder. "Will she live?"

"Maybe, but the bigger question is, how much brain damage did she suffer between the asphyxiation and the head injury, and will she remember anything?"

"Oh."

"She could have been passed out, maybe drugged. But likely we won't know for sure. Chances are good that any drugs have metabolized and are already out of her system. We won't know that for sure until her tox screens come back, but that will take days and we're not holding out hope.

"How do you think she got up in the float?"

"There's that rolling ladder you were using at the garage. That's simple enough. What's not simple is finding someone strong enough to lift 140 pounds of dead weight up the ladder, and slide a limp body in that tube. You know any gorillas that had their library card cancelled lately?"

"Could two people have done it?"

"Could have," Peter agreed, taking a pull on his Beck's. "But who? I thought everyone liked her."

"You have a point. You didn't get anything from the interviews?"

"Nobody knew anything until Sarah dropped in, so to speak. The only way I can make sense of this—the float was headed for Mount Rumpke tomorrow. I suspect her attacker put her there so she'd wind up as landfill. That means they had access to the garage or at least knew Sarah had a key, and they knew that the float was being dumped. This wasn't opportunistic, it was planned."

"But they didn't know enough to know it wasn't strong enough to hold Sarah's weight."

"Nope."

Lia hands were now making large circles on his shoulders. "The ladies didn't say anything else?"

Peter pulled away, turning to look at her. "You know something. What didn't you tell Brent?"

158

Lia sighed and flopped her hands helplessly onto her thighs. "I was sure they'd tell you."

Peter raised one accusing eyebrow.

"Things have been happening."

"What kind of things?"

"You remember when Carol got mugged?"

Peter searched Lia's face. Her eyes were cast down and did not lift to meet his.

They, uh, asked me to look into it."

Peter felt his temper rising.

"And why would they do that?"

"Because they couldn't go to the police?"

Peter ignored the pleading in Lia's voice. He glared at her, saying nothing.

"Look, Leroy's disappearance wasn't a Cincinnati case. I told them to go to the police, but I couldn't force them to come clean, and I didn't know at the time that Brent would be appointed liaison."

Peter's arms were now firmly folded across his chest. "Clean about *what*, exactly? What does Carol's mugging have to do with Leroy?"

Lia spat it out in a rush. "Because-Leroy-wants-more-money-and-they-think-he's-here-and-hunting-them-down."

❦

"Well now, I'm astonished," Brent said, taking a seat at Lia's kitchen table. "You kept vital information about a major crime from the police? Lia, I'm ashamed of you. Pass me a cold one, Brother."

Peter handed Brent a Beck's, remaining silent. Lia knew he was still steaming, but Brent's light tone helped her relax.

"They were just trying to keep Leroy out of trouble. Once he called to let them know he was okay—"

"He WHAT?" Peter blew up.

"Calm down, Brother. I know you'd like to wring her neck right now, but if you can't behave, you'll have to sit out this interview."

"No. No freaking way."

Lia kept her eyes on Brent. "Look, he disappeared again after the phone call."

"Now, why wouldn't they want to tell the Austin police about the phone call?"

"Leroy faked his disappearance to get out of doing a panel at the conference. The Austin police have spent who knows how many thousands of dollars looking for him. Isn't that a crime? Wasting public resources like that?"

"He went to all that trouble to avoid looking ignorant in front of a bunch of for-real writers?" Brent asked.

"He also figured it would be good publicity. The ladies are afraid he'll go to jail. They're also afraid it will get out that he never wrote anything."

"And kill the golden eBook franchise," Brent said.

Lia nodded.

"So you were in on the break in, and you lied to my face about it," Peter said.

"I uh, was the interviewer. The ladies wanted to know for sure if Citrine was involved."

Peter pinched the bridge of his nose and shook his head. "Have I been reborn as Ricky Ricardo? This feels like an episode of 'I Love Lucy.'"

"Would you feel better if I made a Lucy face?"

"NO," Peter and Brent said in unison.

"You sure this isn't an episode of Laverne and Shirley?" Brent asked.

"That would make me Lenny and you Squiggy," Peter pointed out.

Brent shuddered.

"Uh, Is 'Ethel' in on this too?" Brent asked Lia.

Lia nodded.

"'Fred'?"

"Um, yeah."

"Why bring in the hacker?" Brent asked.

Lia glanced at Peter before she responded. His irritation was ebbing as he got caught up in her new information. "That's what started it," Lia said, now on the offensive. "*Somebody* said something to Alma, who told Sarah that I had access to mysterious resources. We were trying to trace Leroy. Trees found pings from the phone in Cincinnati, but no other calls. It was a dead end."

"Now, why," Peter asked, "would someone who was trying to hide leave their phone on so it could be traced?"

"Stupidity?" Lia asked.

"This case has stupidity in it, but it's too-smart-for-your-own-good stupidity, not plain, old-fashioned, stupid stupidity," Peter said.

"Carol takes a fall, Cecilie is drugged and almost drowns, and Sarah is strangled but alive," Brent said. "This murderer of yours is so inept, I feel the urge to trot out a gong."

"I don't get it," Peter said. "If Leroy faked his disappearance, what does that have to do with anything?"

"We don't know where he is now. There may be a bigger plot in motion."

"So the faked disappearance masks a real kidnapping where there is no demand for ransom?" Peter asked.

"Or he fakes his disappearance, sneaks up to murder the group, then reappears after having bribed some Central American cabal to claim they kidnapped him," Lia said.

"Now that's novel," Brent said, "and I do mean that in the worst possible way."

"Why haven't we heard from this cabal?" Peter asked.

"We haven't worked that out yet," Lia pouted.

"Ay-yi-yi-yi-yi," Peter said, shaking his head. "Sorry, I didn't mean that."

"I don't know about you, Brother, but the more Lia tells us, the more confused I get."

"There's only one thing to do." Peter's eyes narrowed dangerously. "Tomorrow we sweat the lady knitters, and I know exactly where to find them."

Chapter 12

Tuesday, July 5

"I don't know what to do," Lia admitted to Bailey, Jim, and Steve from her perch on her usual table. Honey and Chewy were off exploring while Chester and Penny shoved in front of each other to kiss Lia while she dodged their tongues. "I was trying to do the right thing, and I told Peter everything as soon as I knew Fiber and Snark hadn't come clean. He's still furious with me."

"Do you blame him?" Jim asked.

"No." Lia's voice was small. "What do we do now?"

"How much do they know?" Bailey asked.

"Everything."

"Tossed us right under the bus, did you?" Steve asked.

"Maybe not everything. He knows about Citrine and that Bailey and Trees were looking into Leroy's phone. I didn't volunteer anything he didn't already suspect. He doesn't know about the bar hopping."

"I suggest a low profile," Steve said. "What more can we do right now, anyway?"

"I told Sarah last Saturday we were out of it. I think it should stay that way," Lia said.

"What's this I hear? The sound of a thousand clucking chickens?" Terry strolled up with Jackson, having caught the last of the discussion. "If this were Victorian England—"

"Yeah, yeah, we'd be drawn and quartered. Okay, smartie, what do you think we should do?" Steve demanded.

"The pot has been stirred. We need to see what floats to the top," Terry said.

"How do you suggest we do that?" Lia asked.

"Surveillance, of course. If anyone is going to make a mistake, it will be now."

"I can't surveil anything if I want to keep Bonnie happy," Jim said. "She's already decided that you're all a bad influence after yesterday. I'm lucky she allowed me to bring Chester this morning."

"Strike a blow for autonomy, man. Don't let her strangle you with her apron strings," Terry declared.

"My marriage lasted more than 30 years, and it's only over because Mary got cancer. How long did your first wife stay with you?" Jim asked.

"Low blow, my friend, low blow," Terry said.

"But accurate," Steve said. "You have to admit that."

"The cops want us to butt out," Bailey said. "I vote we do that."

"And leave Sarah's downfall to their incompetence?" Terry asked. "What kind of friend would do that?"

Lia's eye's narrowed with annoyance. "We're talking about Peter and Brent, not Heckle and Jeckle. Are you saying that Peter and Brent are incompetent?"

"Well ... I ... ah ...."

"He just wants to do more with that magnifying glass he bought than set ants on fire," Steve said.

Terry's face froze, as if he didn't know whether to be mollified or insulted.

Lia bit her lip. "Peter and Brent are good at their jobs, but they're overworked. I was sure the ladies would tell everything after what happened to Sarah. I don't know why they didn't, but I don't like it. Another thing, listening to Brent run through everything that happened, who's to say it's stopped?"

"You're talking in circles, Lia," Bailey said. "What do you want to do?"

"It was a mistake for me to lie to Peter," Lia said. "Maybe if I hadn't agreed to help, they would have gone to the police. Sarah might never have been attacked. Now that everything is out in the open, I need to let Peter and Brent do their job and stay out of it. You do what you want, follow everyone from here to Timbuktu if you like." She shoved off the picnic table and walked away, towards the back of the park. Honey and Chewy ran to join her.

⁂

Carol sat in the interrogation room, knees together, hands clasped in her lap, cane leaning against the table. She tilted her head and looked up at Brent and Peter with a bland, inquiring look. Every strand of red hair was perfectly fluffed and the powder on her face was dry. She should be sweating in this tiny brick box that was the District Five interview room, but she wasn't.

Catholic School, all 12 years, I bet. Peter scratched his head, affecting confusion. "Help us understand this. Leroy Eberschlag shoves you down a flight of steps tall enough to kill you, and you don't tell me when I arrive on the scene, you don't tell officer Hinkle when he takes your statement, and you don't volunteer this information when your business partner winds up in a coma. Why is that?"

She pursed her lips, looking to the side. Turned back to face Peter, chin up. "I had no proof it was him. What difference does it make?"

"Mrs. Cohn, we know about your business. We know your cabal of knitting cat ladies is the voice behind Lucas Cross, and we know you were at odds with Lucas when he disappeared. With two assaults and an attempted murder tallied against you and your partners, we think the information is critical and find it puzzling that you would leave it out."

"Damn that girl. I knew she couldn't keep a secret."

"Now, don't go blaming Lia, Mrs. Cohn," Brent drawled, laying on his magnolia scented accent. "Peter figured out a long time ago that Leroy didn't write those books."

Carol blinked. "How?"

"We detectives like to detect," Peter said. "It wasn't hard. I understand your desire to keep the public from finding out Leroy is a fake, but we can't understand what's going on if you hide things from us."

"We will be as circumspect as possible, Mrs. Cohn," Brent said. "If it has no bearing on Ms. Schellenger's current condition, we will not disclose it. But we have to consider all possibilities."

"We do have to share this with Austin," Peter said. "There's no way around that."

Carol's face crumpled. She shook her head sadly as she retrieved a kleenex from her purse and dabbed daintily at the corners of her eyes. "All my dreams ... just smoke."

"What do you mean by that, Mrs. Cohn. I thought all the proceeds went to charity," Brent said.

Carol sighed. "That was the original plan. Then we passed the million dollar mark, and we were reconsidering. It was one thing when we were talking about a few thousand dollars. Now we're looking at millions if we can keep it going. That would make all of us comfortable for the rest of our lives."

"When were you going to decide?" Peter asked.

"We were going to sit down after the parade and hammer it out. We need to get it done before the next book launches."

"Who is affected by this?" Brent asked.

"The five of us, Leroy, and our families to a lesser extent. Then there are the charities."

"Who is most affected by any changes?" Peter asked.

"It's questionable - but Leroy was pushing for a partner share. I told him we weren't taking on a new partner unless someone died. It's in our charter, you see. Oh, God, did I give him the idea to kill one of us?" She twisted a kleenex in her hands.

"We don't know that," Brent said. "There's a lot to look at. You've identified a number of people with a stake in the success of the books. Who knew you were going to Clifton the night you were attacked?"

Carol chewed her lipstick off while she thought. "I saw Debby and Alice earlier. I might have mentioned it. Yes, I think I did. But neither of them would be behind this."

Alice scanned the tiny, insufficiently-lit interview room, half of which was taken up by a four-foot table. *The architect should be shot for expecting people to spend time in such a claustrophobic space. Unless that's meant to demoralize suspects. Maybe the architect forgot to put it in and repurposed a utility closet at the last minute.*

"Even if I had a reason to kill Sarah, which I didn't," Alice said, looking over the top of her studious glasses, "I never would have put her body in the float."

"Why is that, Mrs. Emons?" Peter asked.

"I'm an architect. I didn't know Jim McDonald or Jose Mitsch, and I wanted to be sure the float wouldn't fall down and kill someone. It was built well enough, but it was never meant to carry extra weight."

"Wouldn't it have been safer if it had been stronger?" Peter asked.

"Certainly, but a cantilevered structure such as the gun barrel would have required extensive improvements to bear the weight of a full grown adult, and it wasn't worth it for a single use."

"Who knew this, Mrs. Emons?" Brent asked.

"Well, Jerry, it was his trailer and his garage, so he could be held liable. Sarah, she showed me the plans. I don't remember if I said anything to anyone else." Alice frowned and felt a line appearing between her eyebrows. She reminded herself to relax. "But anyone familiar with basic physics would know that the gun barrel would act like a lever if there was weight on the end."

"Is there a chance someone wanted her to fall out in the parade?" Peter asked.

"What a ghastly idea," Alice said. "I hope not. Those poor children will never be the same. The outcome would be impossible to predict. If it fell wrong, it could have landed on somebody."

"So you think we're looking for someone who, say, doesn't know anything about building or engineering?" Peter asked.

"I would agree with that," Alice said.

"What about Leroy Eberschlag?" Brent asked. "Is he familiar with proper construction?"

Alice glanced at her hands. "You'd have to ask Debby or Dorothy, but I suspect not. The only labor he's interested in appears to be lifting beer bottles and picking up women."

"Not about pushing them down steps or trying to drown them?" Peter asked.

Alice sighed and shook her head. "I knew this would never work."

"What is that?" Peter asked.

"Hiding Carol's suspicions about Leroy, that he's in town and stalking us."

"Carol's suspicions? Not yours?" Brent asked. "Didn't he call you from inside Cincinnati?"

"Well, yes, but I only got to listen to his message once before I accidentally deleted it. I'm sure he called in the middle of the night so he could say what he wanted to say and hang up. He certainly didn't threaten us. I honestly don't know what to think."

"Yet you neglected to mention that Leroy was in town when you spoke with us yesterday," Brent said.

"That was for Debby's sake. She couldn't believe he attacked Carol and Cecilie, much less Sarah. Sarah was like family to him."

"What do you think?" Peter asked.

"I don't have enough information to think anything, Detective Dourson. And neither does anyone else."

Cecilie entered the brick closet with the resignation of the red-handed.

"Water, Mrs. Watkins?" Brent asked as she took her seat.

The small woman gave Brent and Peter an embarrassed half smile. She took a sip of water, staring at the glass as she set it back down. "I know what you're going to say."

"What is that?" Peter asked.

"That I should have reported that stupid incident at Twin Towers, and I should have told someone that Leroy might be hanging around."

"We can't argue with that," Brent said. "What stopped you?"

"Leroy is feckless. He doesn't have the drive to be mean. Even when he used to get into bar fights, it was being drunk and stupid. It wasn't rage."

Peter thought back to his prior encounters with Leroy. He couldn't disagree. Leroy's belligerence lacked the vicious edge that kicked your adrenaline into survival mode.

"So what do you think is going on here, if it isn't Leroy?" Peter asked.

"I wasn't sure there was anything until Sarah fell out of the sky and face planted on the pavement in front of me. I knew Leroy was missing, but after the call to Alice, I thought he was whooping it up in Belize."

"Even after you knew the call was placed in Cincinnati?" Peter asked.

"Lia and her friends never found him, did they?"

"Aren't you concerned that someone tried to drown you?" Brent asked.

"But they didn't, not really. There were too many people around. It was a nasty trick, but nothing more than that. I was more upset about spending half the day at the hospital for nothing. I honestly thought Edward was behind it."

"Who's Edward?" Peter asked.

"I don't know why you insisted I come here," Debby said, giving Peter a murderous glare. She yanked a chair out from the table that took up most of the room and sat, arms crossed. Her hair bushed more than usual, giving her a wild look. "The Northside Branch is in a shambles, and my best friend is hanging on by a thread. You should be out looking for the person who did that to her."

"And if that person is your nephew?" Brent asked.

"I don't care what anyone thinks. It's not him," she said.

"Then who is it, Mrs. Carrico?" Peter asked.

"Talk to that Citrine girl. She followed us down the hill. I bet she knew what was going to happen and wanted to watch."

~~~

Peter and Brent watched Debby stomp out of District Five.

"That's one angry woman," Brent said.

"Not angry. Scared. Her nephew is the obvious suspect in an assault on her best friend, and she has no clue where he is," Peter said. "She can't do a thing to help either one of them, and she feels powerless."

"All that from someone who practically spat in your face?"

"Anger is a secondary emotion. If you look for what's under it, you can learn a lot."

"And what did you learn from Mrs. Carrico?" Brent asked. "Do you think she's right about Citrine?"

"Nah. Citrine is harmless. As for Debby Carrico, I vote to move her down the list. But she isn't the one who gave us the most helpful information today."

"Indeed?"

"I think Alice's tidbit about the float is our win for today. We're looking for someone who would benefit from changes in the business, who knew everyone's routines, is strong enough to carry Sarah, and who knew the float was headed for Mount Rumpke, but was not in on conversations about the float's construction."

"Not the inner circle, but one step away?" Brent asked.

Peter nodded. "Husbands."

~~~

Lia sighed at the huge mural overlooking Good Sam's main lobby. Intersecting geometric swoops and stained glass colors combined to remind visitors they were in a religious institution. She wondered how Sarah, with her pagan leanings, would take waking up surrounded by the corporate version of inspirational art. *She'd probably point out that the artist represented Him as a sun god, His face a radiant disk in the sky, far above his worshippers.*

Lia took the elevator to the seventh floor, where she was assured she would find the ICU Family Lounge. The lounge was packed with huddles of worried, resolute, desperate, exhausted, and resigned loved ones. The air smelled of microwave popcorn and burnt coffee.

Fiber and Snark took over a corner in the back. Jerry sat next to Debby, their knees touching, holding hands. Alice had her glasses off and eyes closed, the fingertips of one hand pressed against her forehead. Carol and Cecilie conversed in low tones. There was an empty seat between Alice and Debby, probably reserved for Duane.

Lia crossed the room, winding her way through preoccupied visitors.

"Hello, Lia," Jerry said. "What's that you have, there?"

Lia looked down at the small package in her hand. It was wrapped in plain white tissue and tied with blue ribbon and suddenly seemed insufficient. She quirked an apprehensive half smile. "I thought they might have restrictions about having flowers in the ICU, so I brought Sarah a painting of one that she could keep beside her bed. How is she?"

Alice removed her hand from her forehead and replaced her studious glasses. "Hard to say. She had emergency surgery to relieve pressure on her cranium from internal bleeding. The surgery was successful, but there's no way to tell if she has brain damage until she wakes up. Duane is a mess. He's with her now."

"I'm so sorry." It was the only thing she knew to say, but it was never enough.

Debby looked up, narrowing her eyes. "Did you have to tell your boyfriend about Leroy? We thought you understood what was at stake. We could be ruined."

Lia took a step back. "Don't you want to know who attacked Sarah? You can't expect the police to work in the dark."

"Leroy didn't attack Sarah. They had no reason to know anything about him." She looked as if she would say more, but Jerry put a hand on her arm. Debby looked at him and started to cry.

Cecilie stood up and took Lia by the arm. "Let's take a walk." She led Lia out into the hall, past the chapel with its stained glass portrayal of Mary holding the baby Jesus.

"Things are a mess right now," Cecilie said. "It might be better if you weren't here."

"What was I supposed to do?"

Cecilie raised a hand. "I know, I know. We put you in an impossible position. Some people haven't come around to see that you couldn't do anything else. It will take time. Come on, I'll take you back down." She punched the button on the elevator.

"Cecilie." The hoarse call was full of grief. Lia looked up to see Duane exiting the ICU on the beefy arm of a male nurse. "She's gone. She just went. What am I going to do?"

Cecilie went to Duane and wrapped her arms around the big man. He broke into wailing sobs that brought Sarah's friends running.

Lia's eye's blurred as she watched the nurse help Duane onto a bench, as Sarah's friends closed around him. She felt like a voyeur, intruding as an unwelcome guest on their grief. Lia looked down, her eyes landing on a gift that no longer had a recipient.

The elevator dinged.

Chapter 13

Wednesday, July 6

Peter pulled his third Pepsi of the day from the soft drink machine outside the District Five locker room when he felt a hand like a slab of moose liver land on his shoulder. *Oh, yeah, shift change.*

"Hey, man," Brainard said.

Peter turned, noting the sheepish look on the beefy patrol cop's face. He waited for Brainard to continue.

"I meant to say this a long time ago. Never got the chance."

Peter cocked an eyebrow, saying nothing.

"I just want to apologize for stepping on your turf before."

Peter must have had a confused look on his face, because Brainard rushed to explain. "With Lia, I mean. I didn't know you had a thing going. I just heard she liked badges and thought I'd throw my hat in the ring, her being such a righteous babe and all."

"Liked badges? What, exactly, do you mean by that?" Peter asked. He became conscious of his hand gripping the chilled soda can tightly enough to leave dents. Icy drops of condensation wormed between his fingers.

Brainard flushed. "Aw, you know...." He shrugged, helpless. "I didn't mean any disrespect. I wouldn't poach on a brother."

"I don't know what you heard," Peter said, though he thought he did. "That's my future fiancé you're talking about."

"Aw, man..."

"Anyone who knows anything about Lia, knows I'm the only 'badge' she's ever liked. I wonder why someone would tell you different." Peter wanted to hate the guy, but felt sorry for him instead as he saw the man's brows furrow with his dawning comprehension.

"Damn," Brainard muttered. "Damn!" The big man bit his lip, working his mouth as if considering something weighty. "Look, I have a question for you."

Peter raised his eyebrows.

"I heard this ... rumor awhile back. That some guy was slicing up hookers and dumping them, and the department was keeping it hushed up because they had no clue who was doing it."

"News to me," Peter said.

Brainard deflated. "I was afraid of that. You know when I made an ass out of myself, drawing down on that guy who was just driving to work? That's why. I thought he had a girl in the trunk."

"Rumor, huh?"

"Yeah." Brainard's mouth thinned as his face hardened.

Peter flicked his eyes down to see the man's hands flexing by his side as if he wanted to plow his fists into the wall.

"Gotta watch them rumors," Peter said.

"Oh, I'll be watching them," Brainard narrowed his eyes. "And the birds that spread them. We okay, man?"

"I think we understand each other."

"Yeah, I think we do." Brainard nodded slowly, determinedly, anger glinting behind the slits of his eyes. "We sure do. Uh huh."

As he walked away, Peter wondered what he had just turned loose. *Well, they have it coming.*

What was that about?" Brent asked as Peter returned to their corner of the bullpen. "Captain America looked to be rubbing his two lone brain cells together so fast I expected to see smoke coming out of his ears."

"I expect the rookie figured out that Heckle and Jeckle set him up to get into it with me by telling him Lia was hot for cops." He could imagine it, too, Brainard telling his new buddies about the fine looking woman he'd met on the job and his new buddies stirring the pot by telling him she was one of those women who found a uniform irresistible.

"What *will* you do about that?" Brent's arch inflection made Peter snort. "Or are you going to continue doing nothing?"

"The doe, Grasshopper, has stepped into the clearing. And if I read Brainard right, he's going to shoot it for me."

"I do admire your ability to delegate," Brent said.

Chapter 14

Saturday, July 9

Lia eyed the gravel path leading up the slope of Spring Grove Cemetery's Woodland Walk and sighed.

"I *would* have to wear heels."

"You should be like me," Bailey said, lifting the hem of her floor-length, black sheath. "Birkenstocks for all occasions. Then you're never caught off guard by the need to go off-road."

"They really make your Morticia dress."

"It's the only thing I have in black. I decided to go conventional, though I don't think it was necessary. Look who's officiating."

"Rainbow robes and all," Lia said, spotting the drummer, massage therapist, and non-denominational religious officiant. "Paul gets around. I didn't know Sarah knew him."

"Let's go find Sarah's rock."

Woodland Walk was a more or less natural cremation garden where all the urns were biodegradable and all remains would become one with the land. More or less natural, because the area had been groomed with selective plantings of native wildflowers.

The slope was peppered with boulders. Unlike other grave sites, each plot had its own boulder when it was laid out, which would hold a small bronze plaque. Orange tape and stakes marked future plots for expansion. Going green was trendy.

Lia spotted a piece of red granite with a neat 12 by 12 inch opening in front of it, half way up the hill. She and Bailey strolled up the path to see it.

Bailey knelt in the gravel. "When I go, I want to do it this way, becoming one with the land. I used to think I'd like to be left on a hill for the wolves, but after our experience with the coyotes, I lost my taste for it."

"I'm relieved I won't have to drag your body through Red River Gorge to honor your wishes," Lia said. "I don't know what I want. I never thought about it much until we started attending so many funerals. At one time I thought I would like to be cremated, then have my ashes used in ceramic glaze, so I could become art."

A canopy had been erected at the side of the road, green canvas with a floor of astro-turf. It held a dozen rows of folding chairs. Paul Ravenscraft stood at the head of the tent, talking with Sarah's husband Duane. On a table behind Paul was a modest floral arrangement next to a photo of Sarah with her cats. A notice requested that donations in Sarah's name be made to SCOOP.

"Oh, my," Bailey said, digging an elbow into Lia's side.

"What?"

"Check out the urn. It's a replica of a canopic jar with the head of a cat. Must be made from pressed sand."

Lia suppressed a chuckle. "It's certainly in keeping with all the obelisks in the older sections. Someday they're going to call this Little Egypt."

The tent was packed with library patrons and employees. More people spilled out around it. Lia and Bailey pressed through the crowd. Carol, Debby, Cecilie, and Alice sat in the front row with their husbands. Citrine, her caution-light hipster hair ablaze in a sea of sober colors, was relegated to the third row. She wore a sling on one arm and sat alone, shooting sulky looks at the oblivious crowd.

"Girlfriend looks like she feels out of place," Bailey said.

"Truth."

"We can't see anything from here," Bailey said.

"Let's work our way around to the other side of the tent, up front by Paul, so we can see all the players without being obvious."

The women made a wide circle around the tent and were settling into position when a hand snaked out from the crowd and settled on Lia's shoulder.

She jumped, spinning around to slam her nose into Peter's chest. He ducked his head and whispered in her ear. "Truce, Anderson. Unless you're doing my job?"

"Why would you say that?"

"Looks like you're more interested in the mourners than the service."

"Sarah was my friend. I'm here for her."

"And you picked the best seat in the house if you want to take stock of all the involved parties."

"We can't help it if we got here late," Lia mumbled.

"Uh huh." He raised one eyebrow, looking at her steadily.

"Shhhhh, Paul is about to start." She whipped back around to avoid scrutiny.

Peter moved behind her, keeping a hand on her shoulder, and whispered in her ear. "It's okay. You can be my cover."

Lia snorted. She looked up to see Brent across the tent from her, standing with arms folded, legs planted so the knife-edged creases in his slacks didn't break. He lifted one hand just enough to send her an abbreviated wave, and winked.

She had a moment to wonder why he didn't dress in black more often.

The service opened with remembrances from friends and colleagues. Duane broke down while sharing how meeting Sarah changed his life. Alice represented Fiber and Snark. Lia couldn't help reading into her comments, that they were more about the writing cabal than Sarah's obsession with teddy bear sweaters. Cecilie talked about Sarah's generous service to the feral cat community. A young black man recognized the many ways she supported neighborhood children through her position at the library. Nobody mentioned that she was the guiding force behind millions in ebook sales.

Lia sniffled. Tears rolled down her cheeks. *It's not fair.* She wanted to scream the words. Fun, funny Sarah was gone. A good person died with so much left to give the world.

She came out of her private thoughts to observe the mourners. There wasn't a dry eye in the house, except Citrine, who kept her head bowed in a probable pretense of grief for a woman she barely knew. The front row was a chain of clasped hands and open weeping. Paul's band, Mayan Ruins, stood outside the tent and sang, wordless and ethereal, the sound drifting on the air.

Paul stepped forward and intoned:

Do not stand at my grave and weep.

I am not there; I do not sleep.

I am a thousand winds that blow.

I am the diamond glints on snow.

I am the sunlight on ripened grain.

I am the gentle ...

The crowd began to shift and murmur, drowning out Paul's words. People nudged their companions and lifted chins in Lia's direction. For a moment she panicked. Then she realized they were looking beyond her.

Citrine lifted her head, following the gazes. She shrieked, jumping out of her folding chair. Paul halted his recitation and stood, blinking. Citrine ran out of the tent, both arms waving while her sling hung limp around her neck. The front row gaped, horrified. All attention followed her flight up the hill to the tall figure descending the gravel path.

❧

"Well, I'll be..." Peter muttered.

Leroy Eberschlag met Citrine's out-flung arms with a grimace quickly stifled as he accepted her hug. Peter wondered how many people noticed the quick flash of annoyance and the subtle way he peeled her off, using his tight grip on her hand to move her to the side so that he was dragging her down the hill.

Way to ruin his entrance, Citrine.

Citrine was pushed out of the way by Debby and her sister, Dorothy, who fell on him sobbing and crying "Praise the Lord," over and over. Peter noticed cell phones emerging from pockets and imagined photos of the return of Lucas Cross were already going viral.

Paul stood patiently as Debby booted someone out of their chair at the end of the second row and dragged it around so that she and her sister could sandwich Leroy between them. The crowd eventually settled and Paul began again. The crowd shifted and stared, but kept the murmuring to a minimum.

Brent lifted an eyebrow to Peter. Peter's chin brushed Lia's hair as he sent a quick shake of his head back.

"What are you going to do?" Lia whispered to Peter.

"I'm going to have some respect. He's not going anywhere. We'll pick him up before the media gets here. I don't know how long we'll be. I'll call you later and let you know, once we figure out what the hell is going on."

"Don't worry about the time. Just come over if you're not too tired after you finish up."

Paul's sermon complete, Duane came forward to pick up Sarah's urn, following Paul to the path up the hillside. The mourners followed, emptying their seats by rows. Peter and Brent cut neatly into the line behind the family. The procession headed up the hillside, winding around to follow the gravel path through the garden, reminding Lia of a time when Paul led a conga line at a party.

The line of mourners snaked along the path, until they reached the boulder of red granite and the tiny grave in front of it. Mayan Ruins sang while Duane lowered the urn into the grave and sprinkled a handful of dirt on it. A select number of family and friends stepped forward to sprinkle more dirt into the grave, then stood by with bowed heads as the band finished their tribute.

Mourners clogged the paths, making it impossible for Paul and Duane to return down the hill the way they came. There were a few minutes of jockeying until it became apparent that the line should now proceed forward to pay respects to Duane by the graveside.

Peter and Brent stayed several feet behind Leroy until he shared his condolences, then moved forward to interrupt the Eberschlag family reunion.

Leroy and Dorothy gave the detectives quizzical looks. Debby just sighed in resignation.

"You taking him?" she asked.

"We need to ask Mr. Eberschlag a few questions, if you don't mind," Peter said.

"What is this?" Leroy asked.

"I'm Detective Dourson with the Cincinnati Police, and this is my partner, Detective Davis. I'm sure you know a lot of people have been looking for you. It would be best if we got out of here before the reporters show up."

"I don't mind reporters," Leroy said.

"We do," Brent said.

"Where are you taking him?" Dorothy cried, hanging onto Leroy's arm. "I just got him back!"

"Ma, don't make a scene," Leroy said.

"District Five. We'll have someone bring him home when we're done," Peter said.

"No," Dorothy said. "I'll follow you, and I'll wait."

"Ma, you don't need to do that."

"Yes, I do, and you'd know that if you'd bothered to grow up and have children of your own."

"Ma'am," Brent said, tipping his head, "this could take a long time. It would be better for you to go home."

"You going now?" Debby asked.

"Yes ma'am," Brent said.

"Hold up a minute." She took two steps to get within hugging distance of Leroy, then smacked him on the back of his head. "That's for worrying your ma and me to death."

Peter stared at a half-sheepish, half-smirking Leroy sitting across from him in the interview room. Leroy was a tall man, and slouched in his chair in a way that suggested it was too small for him. He had longish dark hair in disordered waves and strong white teeth that a crooked incisor saved from looking fake. Mother nature gave him a dazzling smile. Even when he was smirking, it came off as good natured.

Brent leaned against the brick wall. Peter knew he could see behind the table from his position, and was taking note of any nervous gestures Leroy made.

"You expect us to believe that Kat Dennings kidnapped you at AustinCon and kept you prisoner for four weeks?" Peter asked, eyebrows raised to their upper limit.

"Hey, man, I'm not that dumb. I said she looked like Kat Dennings, and told me to call her Kat, probably, you know, because she looked like her. And I wasn't exactly trying to escape, if you know what I mean."

"Who's Kat Dennings?" Brent asked.

"The girl on the TV show, the waitresses who bake cupcakes," Leroy said.

"You watch that?" Brent asked, incredulous.

"No, man. My ma does. Never misses it. But the chick is hot, like die happy hot. Dark, wavy hair, a rack out to here—" Leroy paused to demonstrate with his hands. "—and these smoky grey eyes with a look in them like she knows she could teach you a thing or two. She does this thing with her eyebrow, it kills me. Then there's that mouth."

"See, what we don't understand, is how, if you were chained up in an RV a thousand miles away, you managed to transport yourself to Cincinnati to leave a message on Alice Emon's phone," Peter explained.

Leroy jumped out of his chair. "What the hell are you talking about? I haven't spoken to anyone for a month."

"Is Alice Emons a liar?" Brent asked.

"Alice? She's a good lady," Leroy said.

"Alice states she found a message from you on her phone one morning," Brent said. "In it, you told her that you were in Belize—"

"WHAT?"

"—And that you faked your disappearance so that you would not be revealed as a charlatan, and to boost sales of your books. We traced the number and found it was a pre-paid cell phone purchased and activated in Austin and pinging along highways all the way to Cincinnati, where it's been pinging on the west side of town ever since."

"Now, wait a minute—"

"Hold your horses, Hoss," Brent said. "Settle down. We want to keep this friendly for the nice camera." Brent nodded at the video cam mounted near the ceiling.

"Aw, c'mon! Do I look that dumb?" Leroy said. "That's like leaving breadcrumbs."

"We'll let you in on a little secret," Brent said. "Nobody you know is nominating you for the Nobel Prize."

Leroy slumped back in his chair and huffed. "I don't freaking believe this. Where is this message? I want to hear it."

"The message was deleted and could not be recovered," Peter said.

"Oh, *that's* handy," Leroy scoffed.

"Tell us again where you've been staying, Leroy," Peter said. "Those pings put you in the right place on the days someone attempted to kill two of your—" Here Peter hooked his fingers to make air quotes. "—ghostwriters."

"Then there was July 3rd, when *someone* attacked Sarah and left her for dead," Brent added.

"Now that's downright stupid. Someone is trying to frame me!"

"From where I'm sitting," Brent drawled. "They're succeeding."

"Tell us again from the beginning," Peter said.

"Look, I was signing books, and this chick walks up and leans over my table, right in front of me, and I can see all the way to China, where she has this little tattoo. She says she has a present for me, and she does that thing with her eyebrow, like Kat Dennings. She leaves me this bag, and it has an Arab robe-thing in it and a bunch of instructions. It sounded kinky, so I went for it, and met her down in the basement that night like she asked. She pulled a gun on me and made me get in the back of a van and handcuffed me."

"And she kept you tied up in an RV and forced you to rewrite one of your characters?"

"Chained up. Handcuff on my left hand." Leroy rubbed that wrist unconsciously. "The other end of the handcuff ran through a link on a chain that was bolted to the floor. She said she hated how I did Koi, said I didn't get some feminist bullshit about female rage, and I was going to write a new Koi book. If she liked what I wrote, she would reward me, and if she didn't like what I wrote, she was going to punish me. Only she was wearing this leather shit, and sometimes she made me wear a ball gag so I couldn't yell for help. The rest of the time we were somewhere flat, where there wasn't anything for miles around, West Texas or Arizona maybe. Some desert. She said I could scream my head off if I wanted. I expected some kink, but this was out there."

"I remember that movie. Stephen King, wasn't it, Brent?"

"Yeah...I think so...only it was Kathy Bates, and there was no leather involved. I've never seen a movie where a beautiful woman takes a writer captive and exchanges sexual favors for writing." Brent cocked his head and examined Leroy's legs. "I don't see casts on his ankles. You see casts on his ankles?"

"He did say he wasn't trying too hard to escape. James Caan tried to escape."

"Who wouldn't try to escape from Kathy Bates? She was nuts. I don't think she did anything cute with her eyebrow, either."

Peter crossed his arms and shook his head, sighing. "I don't think it happened. What do you think, Brent?"

"No, no, man. It happened just like I said," Leroy pleaded.

"There's a problem with your story," Peter said, "and it isn't your sit-com fantasy girl. We know you don't write your books. So how can you spend a month writing in an RV when everyone says you're one step up from illiterate?"

Leroy looked embarrassed. "Look, nobody knows this, but I've been studying up. After running around pretending to be a writer, I got to thinking I could really do it. I got story ideas and everything. There's this guy, James Patterson. You ever hear of him?"

Peter and Brent gave him blank looks of incredulity.

"Really! He's this writer and he has this Master Class online. He says he'll teach you everything he knows about writing best sellers for $90. The dude's had nineteen number one best sellers in a row! Boom, boom, boom!" He chopped his hand in the air to punctuate each 'boom.' "Like that. You can check it out. So I've been studying."

"This is so very sad," Brent said.

"Hey, victim here!" Leroy yelled.

"So you say," Peter said. "And she let you go to Sarah's funeral, what, out of the goodness of her heart? Time off for good behavior?"

"I think, after she read Leroy's stuff, she chewed his arm off so he could get away," Brent said.

"She did! I mean, she didn't chew my arm off. You can see I still have it. Them. I still have both of them." Leroy raised his arms to demonstrate. "She let me go. Look, she was following all that stuff on the internet whenever we hit town, you know, the police search and what people were saying, and how my book sales were going through the roof." Leroy got a disgusted look on his face. "And if I ever see that Citrine chick again, I'm getting a restraining order. Kat used to read all these sappy things Citrine claimed I did and said, and she'd fall over laughing. I only bounced on that chick a couple times, and now she's all *Fatal Attraction*."

"Now we're back with the movies." Peter leaned forward with his hands on his knees, crowding Leroy. "How did you wind up at the cemetery?"

"I'm getting to that. A couple times a week, she'd drive into some truck stop—"

"How did you know it was a truck stop if you were chained up in a room with the windows covered?"

"It was just off the highway, and I could hear the rigs pulling in." Leroy gave Brent a "duh" look. "She'd hook into the wifi and download a ton of stuff while she got us food to go—she'd say she wanted something besides the microwave junk we had in the RV—mine was always cold because she wouldn't take the ball gag out until we were out in nowhere again.

"She read about Sarah online. You know, about falling out of the float in the parade, and she's laughing at how crazy it was until I tell her she's my aunt's best friend. She got this funny look on her face and says she's making an executive decision. She starts driving and I don't know where the hell we are because the windows in my room are blacked out, but she's driving, like 12 hours a day.

"Today she tells me to clean up, and she's washed my clothes, and a couple hours later, she dumps me at the back gate of the cemetery with a map she printed out with an "X" for Sarah's funeral, and just drives off." He pulled a folded piece of paper out of his pocket and laid it on the little table.

"Dammit," Brent slammed his palm on the side table. "She's had a two hour head start by now. What kind of RV was it? We'll get a BOLO out."

"Won't do you any good. She said she was ditching it and you'd never find her."

"What do you think?" Brent asked, looking at Peter.

"So you believe me now?" Leroy asked, hope etched on his face.

"Tell us about the RV," Peter said. "And the tattoo."

"She wasn't a bad chick." Leroy snorted, a sad, self-derisive snort, and looked at his hands. "I'm gonna miss her, you know?"

"That's so sweet," Brent said. "We're going through your story again, but this time you're going to do it backwards."

Peter rubbed his jaw, the harsh rasp of stubble telling him they'd been at it too long. *Dammit. I never called Lia.* He looked at the clock. They'd had Eberschlag in the box for more than six hours. He supposed he should be grateful Lia took it in stride when work interfered with their plans, but part of him wished she didn't get along so well without him.

"Leroy, where do you want to go tonight? Home or your mother's?" he asked.

"I'd better go to Ma's. After a month of thinking I might be dead, she'd kill me herself if I didn't go see her first. And knowing her, she's been cooking. I'm sick of microwave dinners."

The sight of TV news vans camped outside Dorothy Eberschlag's house had Leroy rethinking his plan to see his mother. He ducked down in Peter's Explorer as they drove past the mob of reporters. Peter drove around the corner, took a quick left and went down two blocks to Debby's house. The house was dark.

"It's okay," Leroy said. "I bet they're all at Ma's. I know where the spare key is. I'll call everyone when I'm inside. Then I'm taking the world's longest shower."

"What do you think?" Brent asked Peter, as they watched Leroy disappear into Debby's house.

Peter started up his Explorer and pulled out of the drive. "I think it's funny Ms. X said she was making an executive decision. People usually say that when there's someone else in charge and they've decided to take things into their own hands. Leroy isn't subtle enough to make that detail up if it was part of his story. Instead, he'd tell us she was talking to someone on the phone, or texting her boss."

"She said it after she found out Sarah died, and what her relationship to Leroy was. Whatever was going on, maybe she figured things had gone too far. Why do you suppose she brought him all the way back here?"

"Remorse?" Peter said. "That, or the game was always supposed to end here, and this was where her exit strategy was set up."

"What exit strategy?"

"Dunno. If she had a full tank and a siphon, all she'd have to do is drive outside town and set it on fire. Then she picks up a car she has stashed, or someone meets her."

"Or she does it out off I-275, then hoofs it to the air-port and rents a car. Which is better, since that's in Ken-tucky."

"True. Or she drives back to Grandpa's in Illinois and thanks him for loaning it to her."

"We don't have the plate number. Do we send out a BOLO with Kat Dennings' picture on it?"

"We'd never hear the end of it. But just in case, let's ask dispatch to alert us if any RVs explode."

"Who do you think her boss is?"

"Better question is, where did they find her? She has to have some skills to pull the whole thing off."

"Online dominatrix?"

"Are you volunteering to research that option?"

"I'm always willing to take one for the team. You know that."

"Uh huh. I'll hand it off to Cynth. She's less likely to get distracted."

Brent sighed. "You sure know how to take all the fun out of this job."

"Six hours with Leroy Eberschlag wasn't you're idea of a good time?"

"Only when he looked like he was going to wet his pants. We never did get into what kind of punishments and rewards she gave him."

"Some things are better left to the imagination."

"I imagine you're right. Someone set up a scheme so nutty, when Leroy returns, he tells us a story so ridiculous, anyone in their right mind wouldn't believe it. Meanwhile, the only tracks we can find place him in Cincinnati on the crucial dates. If he was pretending to be kidnapped, why would he use a phone?"

"He wouldn't. Every four year old knows phones can be traced."

"Wouldn't our real killer know that? Maybe Leroy created the too-obvious frame job to fake us out."

"Six hours in there, and we couldn't shake his story," Peter reminded him.

"He's had a month to rehearse it."

Peter shook his head. "You'd have to be a total psychopath to fake the reaction he had when we told him about the pings. Leroy's a wuss. If he was lying, we would have broken him in half an hour."

"He's been faking this author schtick for a couple years now. I imagine he's learned to think fast," Brent said.

"I think we'd do better to look at people who we already know have been lying to us."

"The knitting club?"

"Maybe their third time in interview will be the charm, but let's do it tomorrow."

"The trouble is, anyone could have been behind it. It's the big question we have to answer," Brent said.

"Yeah," Peter said. "Who put Sarah in the gun barrel?"

Stealthy movements invaded Lia's dreams. She drifted into consciousness, rolling onto her side and peering into the dark. A figure moved in and out of the shaft of moonlight slipping between the curtains. Disembodied hands moved deftly down, unbuttoning a shirt.

"Hey there, Kentucky Boy."

"Hey yourself. I was trying not to wake you."

"And miss the striptease? I don't think so."

"And here my best g-string is in the laundry."

"I'll live. Drop those slacks and crawl in here."

"If you insist." He sat down on the edge of the bed and pulled off one shoe, tossing it in the air with a rakish flair. It fell to the floor with a thump that roused all three dogs from their sleep on the far side of the bed. Viola crawled across the covers to Peter and sniffed him suspiciously, as if he'd been with another dog, then settled her head on his thigh for a pet.

"Aw, look, you woke up the children."

Peter looked down at Viola and sighed. "You sure know how to spoil the mood."

Viola craned her head up and flicked her tongue across his nose. He stroked her with the feather-light touch she preferred, then stood up and opened the bedroom door. "Okay, kids, Mom and Dad need some alone time."

Viola cocked her head as if he'd been speaking Mongolian and Honey dropped her muzzle, pretending to be asleep. Chewy snugged his nose under Lia's hand, hoping for a scratch.

"OUT!" Peter pointed into the hall and the dogs made a dash for the living room. Viola lingered in the doorway, looking hurt. "You, too, Princess."

Lia felt a tug on her heart as Viola slunk away. "You're such a guy. You could at least give them treats if you're going to toss them out of a warm bed."

"Man sleep on bed. Dog sleep on floor. Man speak. Dog listen. Ugh." Peter punctuated this pronouncement with a thump on his chest.

"Yeah, that will work."

"You could at least let me pretend I'm in charge. Think of my poor battered male ego here."

"Uh huh. You've been reading John Grey again, haven't you?"

Peter dropped his other shoe on the floor, then stood up and stepped out of his slacks. He shook them out and hung them over the back of a chair whose only purpose was holding Peter's clothes when he spent the night. His shirt came next. He draped it around the back of the chair like a hanger, then followed by laying his undershirt, briefs, and socks across the seat. Lia shook her head.

"Such a boy scout."

Peter slid under the covers and over her, caging Lia's face between his forearms. "Eagle scout." He bent down to kiss her.

"Mmmm." Lia put a restraining hand on his chest.

"What?"

"I know it's been a long day for you, but I can't stand it. I won't be able to think about anything else until you tell me where Leroy has been all this time."

"Well, damn." He flopped over on his back. Lia placed her head on his shoulder and he curved his arm around her. She traced a finger down his chest. "Please? Pretty, pretty pretty please, with butter and maple syrup on top? And sprinkled with pecans?"

"Does that come with sexual favors?"

"That depends on the quality of your intel." She kissed his neck. "They've been running video clips from the funeral on television all night. The mysterious return of Lucas Cross, AKA Leroy Eberschlag, is all over the internet. Sleeping with a detective has to have some benefits. Gimme."

He tapped her lips with his index finger, which she nipped. "And what happens when you see Bailey at the park tomorrow, and she says having a friend sleeping with a detective should have benefits?"

"Oh. I didn't know you wanted to sleep." Lia rolled over on her other side and proceeded to snore.

Peter goosed her, pulling her back over when she yelped. "Pinky swear you won't tell anyone until I say it's okay?" He held out his hand with the little finger crooked.

Lia crooked her little finger around his and wiggled it. "Pinky swear. Sure you don't want to do a blood oath?"

"This is good enough." He gave her the short version of Leroy's story.

"That's crazy. I can't believe he thinks you'd buy it."

Peter scratched his head with his free hand. "That's the thing. It feels like he's telling the truth. Everything about his body language says he was being totally honest."

"He was kept prisoner in the desert by a dominatrix who made him write, and she punished him when it wasn't good enough? What was the punishment?"

"We didn't nail down that detail. We were more concerned with a description of the RV."

"But that's the best part!"

"Guy's twisted up. I think he's got Stockholm syndrome."

"He's in love with his kidnapper?"

"From what he said, she's really hot."

Lia scoffed. "Men will take any kind of abuse from a female, as long as she's hot. What about the phone call?"

"He denies having the phone and doesn't know who made it."

"What about his keeper? Could she have done it?"

"Possibly. I would say probably, except that would mean he was lying about being out west. Why would he do that?"

"Sarah said he was a total bullshitter and that's why he was so good at pretending to be an author. Maybe he faked you out."

"There's a difference between the guy who tells stories at a bar and a psychopath who can fool people he's known all his life. Chances are, if he was a psychopath, he wouldn't have a reputation for being a bullshitter."

"So you think he was set up."

"It's stupidly elaborate, but it makes a bizarre kind of sense."

"But why? Who would want to kill Sarah? Everyone loved her."

"People kill for passion, self-protection, and greed. When you have something that's plotted out in advance, I always vote for greed. In this case, I'll be damned if I can figure out how someone else benefitted by killing her. Even Leroy's supposed motive is thin."

"Cui bono? Isn't that the latin legalese for 'who benefits'? That's what Terry says."

Peter tapped the dent in her chin. "You really want to talk about this now?"

Lia leaned her head on Peter's shoulder and drew a finger down his chest, into the expanse of dark curls. She drew circles with her finger, forging trails across his forested pecs.

"You know it tickles when you do that."

"Uh huh. Don't let it distract you. So what changed when Sarah died?"

Peter looked up at the ceiling. "Let's see. Bang Bang Books automatically dissolved and they have to re-form their business. They could bring in new partners or change the distribution of profits.

"Duane is widowed. If anyone has the hots for him, he's available. I don't think Duane is behind it. Not only is he incapable because of his back, the contract on the house they were buying is void and he can't swing the loan without Sarah's income. He's stuck with a condo he hates and a financial mess. If he was behind it, he would have waited until the mortgage insurance kicked in after the closing."

"Won't he inherit her share of the business?" Lia said.

"The way I understand it, her share is what's divided up after they funnel most of it out to charity, and with the LLC dissolving, there is no more share for Sarah, except what remains from the dissolution of the LLC. Peter stared at the ceiling, thinking. "He's probably entitled to a share of the copyrights, and that could turn into something eventually.

"SCOOP lost their biggest supporter. I had the impression that if someone wanted Bang Bang Books to stop donating money to animal rescue organizations, they'd have to get Sarah out of the way first.

"Then there's creative control. In a group like that, you can have a lot of ego. The bigger the money gets, the higher the stakes, the tenser the situation can get. Cracks form. Jealousy and competition sneak in. Look at Yoko Ono and the Beatles. Mike Love and Brian Wilson. Diana Ross and the Supremes," Peter concluded.

"This is like a band, isn't it?"

"Without the drugs."

"True," Lia said.

"You've been around the ladies a lot. Did you ever get the sense anyone felt they were being dismissed? Maybe not anyone in the group, but around them?"

"There's Citrine, but I don't think she could pull something like this off, and I suspect her connection with Leroy is really thin. Killing Sarah wouldn't make sense. If Citrine went after anyone, it would be Debby."

"What about Leroy?"

"They didn't seem to take him seriously. Half the group thinks he's behind everything, the rest thinks he doesn't have the brains to pull it off. I haven't talked to anyone since he got back, so I don't know if that's changed."

"It's possible Leroy made the whole kidnapping bit up to give himself an alibi while he ran around attacking the women," Peter said.

"But without Sarah, I don't know if the group can hang together. She was the glue. He would know that."

"Someone attacked Carol and Cecilie first. He could have gotten desperate after he failed with them and with time running out on his little sabbatical, he needed to take advantage of the next opportunity he had. That's if he did it to get the LLC to open up before his next launch."

"Is that your current theory?"

"It's the one that makes sense."

"And how does the crazed dominatrix-slash-fan fit in?" Lia asked.

"The guy has to have a story that explains why he was kidnapped and held so long and no one asked for ransom. The stalker is the best fit," Peter said.

"So you think it was Leroy."

"He tells a believable story, but the more I think about it, the more I like him for Sarah's murder. I think it's time to get into Bang Bang Books's finances."

Lia rolled over, on top of Peter. "And I think it's time to get into something else."

Chapter 15

Tuesday July 12

"Lia know about your new girlfriend, Dourson?" Hodgkins asked. He and Jarvis blocked the door to the bullpen.

"Maybe someone should tell her," Jarvis said. "You know, because there are diseases and things."

"What the hell are you talking about?"

"She's sitting at your desk. Said she'd only talk to you. Davis is keeping her company, but she's not biting. Guess she doesn't go for metro-idiots."

"You mean faggots," Jarvis said.

"That too," Hodgkins agreed, grinning.

Peter stifled his irritation and pushed between them. The woman sitting at his desk must have taken her wardrobe tips from Cynth. The baggy smock and cropped dojo pants couldn't disguise the brick bombshell body hiding underneath.

Lustrous black hair bundled on top of her head, held in place with a pair of short chop sticks, which he didn't know was a thing until he met Lia. Sunglasses hid her eyes. She wore no make up. Peter thought she didn't realize her mouth looked so much more vulnerable and tender without the siren-red lipstick he suspected she usually wore.

She held her knees together while her hands worried a soda can in her lap in a way that suggested she liked to scratch labels off of beer bottles when she was nervous. Closer inspection revealed fretful crinkles in her forehead. Brent sat on the corner of his desk, likely chattering away about nothing to keep her comfortable.

"And here he is," Brent said, nodding to Peter.

She looked up, her face stiffening. With resolve? Defiance? *She doesn't want to be here. Well, most people don't.*

Peter nodded pleasantly. "I guess we need an interview room."

"We do, indeed. Shall we?" Brent cocked his head at the moused-up vamp. A smile of acquiescence flicked across her face. She slung a hobo bag the size of Montana over one shoulder and gripped her diet Pepsi as if her life depended on it. "Let's," she said in a voice like velvet and smoke.

The woman followed Brent back while Peter took up the rear, cataloguing a dozen different impressions. He found the contrast between the assured voice and the obvious nerves intriguing. Her feet were pampered and her carriage graceful. *A dancer? She does something physical.* The canvas gladiator sandals were both casual and sexy.

Peter closed the door to the interview room and turned to face her. She sat at the table, head tilted down, worrying her lips. *Used to chewing off her lipstick.*

"Kat is it?"

"Linda, actually. Linda Lyle." She lifted her head and removed the sunglasses to reveal eyes as smokey and soft as her voice. "So he told you?"

"Who told us what, Linda?" Brent asked.

"Leroy. That I kidnapped him and held him prisoner for four weeks in the desert. I wanted you to know there was no way he could have killed that woman."

"What brought you here, Linda?" Peter asked.

"Look, I stay on the right side of the law ..."

"Seriously?" Brent mocked.

Peter waved him off. "Let her explain."

"I have a fantasy business, based in LA. I'm a dominatrix. No sex. It's not prostitution. I do scenarios."

Peter tilted his head and quirked an eyebrow.

"You wouldn't believe what hot shots will pay me to beat them and make them clean my house. I've got the cleanest grout west of the Mayo Clinic."

"Everyone has to make a living," Brent drawled.

"How did you get into that?" Peter asked.

"Went to Hollywood and didn't know Kat Dennings was around. I looked too much like her to ever make it as an actress, but I got solicited to do look-alike gigs for singing telegrams. Then someone asked me if I did fantasy scenarios. The dominatrix gig paid the best money."

"I'll bet," Brent said.

"Is he going to continue sneering at me? I make an honest living and I came in on my own. I was out of here, free and clear, and I came back."

Peter raised his eyebrows and looked at Brent.

"My apologies," Brent said. "Please proceed."

"Back in April, I got an email offering me $100,000 for a four week gig. I copied off all the email communication, the contract, and bank info for you." She laid a thumb drive on the table. "I want you to know this was a straight up business contract."

"Do you often conduct business by email?"

"That's most of it. Email and bank transfers. These bank transfers came from the Caymans."

"That didn't worry you?"

She shook her head. "Most of my clients want to keep our business private. They don't want records of payments where they can be traced. I can't blame them, can you?"

"So tracing the payments would be a dead end," Peter said.

"Cynth could take a look at the emails," Brent said. "What was the nature of this gig?"

"He said his name was Lucas Cross, and he needed help breaking out of a bad case of writer's block. Said he had stage fright because he'd been contracted by a major publisher willing to pay millions for a new book. I was supposed to kidnap him from this writer's conference, chain him up in the RV and keep him out in the middle of nowhere for four weeks so he could get out his first draft. There were a number of stipulations, but the main one was that I never break out of character."

Peter rubbed his forehead. "Weird, but I guess it's not illegal, if that's what went down."

"Perhaps we need to bring Leroy back in for a chat," Brent said. "What you did may be legal, but perpetuating a fraud on the public isn't, not when hundreds of thousands of dollars in taxpayer money were spent searching for him."

"But that's just it," Linda said, squeezing the Pepsi can so tight, it crinkled. "I don't think it was Luke who booked me. He's a decent guy. I don't want him to get in any trouble."

"Interesting," Brent said. "Who do you think it was?"

"I have no idea."

"What made you think it wasn't Lucas?" Peter asked.

"When that woman died, falling out of his float. He freaked. I knew then, whether he was paying me or not, something else was going on and I didn't want to be part of it. I hauled ass back here. I thought the least I could do was get him to her funeral, since she seemed important to him. I figured all hell was going to break out after that."

"It has, indeed," Brent said.

"He didn't question it when I hit the interstate. I knew for sure then. We still had a few days left on his dime, and the contract stated I would drop him at a bar in Austin when his time was up. If he'd booked me, he would have said something.

"Am I in trouble?"

"That's a good question," Peter said. "We have to call Austin."

"I was afraid you'd say that." She bit her lip, looking at Brent and Peter with a bleak expression.

"Can you stay in town until we sort this out?"

"I can stay a few days, at least. I hear there's a decent RV park west of town."

"What do you think?" Brent asked as they watched Linda climb into her RV.

"I think I need a beer."

"So do I. Too bad it's only eleven."

"If this doesn't bring back memories," Brent said as he climbed onto the stair stepper next to Cynth's after he went off duty. McKie Recreation Center was little more than a mile from the station and was popular with District Five.

"I recall you were on this very same machine the first time I laid eyes on you. Time stood still as I realized that I would never be graced with the presence of a more magnificent woman."

Cynth rolled her eyes while maintaining her rhythm. "You just don't quit, do you?"

"I know what I want, and I know, deep down, you want it too."

"My little cousin wants to run out into the street every time he hears a car coming. His daddy wants a drink every morning when he wakes up. Want is just an urge. A meaningless firing of neurons that has no understanding of what is good for you."

Brent turned serious. "You're more than an urge. We almost had something going, back when. I've never forgotten how it was. Don't you feel the unfinished business between us?"

"The only--"

A howl of pain erupted from the weight room. Brent and Cynth jumped off their machines and dashed through the door in tandem, as if they were long-time partners. Brent felt a brief and painful stab of nostalgia at the way they just clicked.

Jarvis, AKA Jeckle, lay pinned on a weight bench, a barbell across his chest, loaded with what Brent estimated to be 250 pounds of plates.

"Goddammit, get this off me," Jarvis yelled, his face a dangerous red.

"I think I sprained my wrist," Brainard whined, supporting the injured joint with his other hand. "Sorry man."

Brent could only see a sliver of Brainard's face, but he thought he caught a fierce grin.

Cynth reached the bench first. Brent ran around to the other side, and together they lifted the weight off Jarvis' chest and settled it into the rack over the bench.

"Don't move," Cynth said. "How do you feel?"

"How do you think I feel after this *oaf* dropped the bar while he was spotting me?"

"Hey," Brainard protested. "I told you it wasn't a good idea to load on the plates like that."

"Settle down," Cynth said. "Does it hurt when you breathe?"

Jarvis wheezed. "I think my sternum is cracked."

Cynth patted her waist for a cell phone that wasn't there. "I'm going to go call for an ambulance."

As soon as she left the room, Jeckle's eyes narrowed and his face grew even redder. "You did that on purpose," he said.

Brainard's eyebrows rose. "You mean like you neglected to tell me Lia Anderson was Peter's woman on purpose? Like you and Hodgkins made up that story about the East Side Slasher on purpose, so I nearly shot a civilian while you watched? And wound up getting a new one ripped by Roller? I bet you and Hodgkins got a big laugh out of that. We got a new captain coming in, and I got a blot on my record. You think that's funny?"

"You're dead," Jarvis spat out.

Brainard let go of his "sprained" wrist and placed the palm of that hand on the center of Jarvis' chest. He leaned in until Jarvis' face turned white with pain as he gasped like a beached guppie.

"Ease off, man, you'll hurt that wrist even more," Brent said quickly as Cynth re-entered the weight room. "Why don't you take a seat while we wait for the EMTs?"

Jeckle was packed off to Good Sam while Brainard pulled a doleful face full of self-recrimination. Brent had to admire his acting ability and decided that maybe Brainard was smarter than he looked. Not by much, mind you, but at least by enough to allow Cynth to continue believing Jeckle's injury was an accident.

Cynth returned from escorting the EMTs out of the rec center and zeroed in on Brainard's dangling arm. "Why didn't you have that seen to while the medics were here? Let me have a look at it."

Brainard held his good hand up, palm out, to stop her. "You've done enough. I'll ice it when I get home and wrap it up. I saw way worse in Afghanistan. I gotta get going. See you, man." He fist bumped Brent with his good hand and headed for the door.

"How are you going to drive one handed?" Cynth demanded.

Brainard looked back. "Don't you know? I'm Captain America. I think I'll manage." He sauntered out of the room, Cynth eying him suspiciously.

"You can look at my hand, if you like," Brent said to distract her. "I think I scraped my knuckles getting that weight off Jeckle's chest."

Cynth rolled her eyes as she let out a frustrated "huh" and walked off. Brent watched her long braid swing above her very toned glutes as she headed for the locker room.

"Oh, darlin'," he mourned.

Chapter 16

Wednesday, July 13

Peter arrived with dinner balanced on top of a four-inch binder stuffed with papers. Lia took Viola's leash and held the door for him.

"Who rang the bell? Viola?"

"I used my elbow."

"Good thinking." She leaned over and sniffed the bags. The dogs sat and whined. "You've all had your dinner—Chinese?"

"I figure you've got to be craving pasta after all these weeks without it. The chow fun is made with rice noodles, no wheat. We also have teriyaki beef, and shrimp with broccoli. All diet approved. I already ate your fortune cookie so you wouldn't be tempted. It said you're going to spend a romantic evening with a tall, dark, incredibly handsome man tonight."

"Yum. Food sounds good, too. What's the binder? Homework?"

"It's Sarah's murder book."

"All that?"

"And a bag of chips. I need to spend some time with it this evening."

"I can't believe one murder generates that much paper."

"I wish this one didn't."

Peter set his load down on the kitchen counter and unpacked the bags while Lia took dishes out of the cabinet. "This case is so crazy, it's hard to see what's really going on." He took a plate, using two forks to load it with the skinny noodles on one half, then spooned beef and shrimp on the other side and handed it to Lia. He filled a second plate for himself and took a seat at the table.

The dogs sat, eyes glued to this entire process.

"What has you hung up?" Lia asked, ignoring them. Viola curled under Peter's chair with her head on her paws and sighed. Honey padded away, grumbling. Chewy waited, ever hopeful for a dropped morsel.

Peter made a face, then speared a shrimp.

"That bad?"

"Where do I start?" Peter ticked off points on his fingers. "Since Sarah didn't die during the attack, we can't pinpoint when it happened. Our window of opportunity is more than 10 hours. That makes it hard to rule anyone out.

"The people with the most motive would be Leroy and his cabal of knitting librarians, but unless RV lady is a scam, Leroy is accounted for and none of those women are strong enough to get Sarah inside the float. Not unless they all ganged up on her, and I can't see that. Even if I could, their time frames don't align. And if it was a conspiracy, one of them would have cracked by now.

"We can't identify the murder weapon. We thought it was some kind of horse halter, but we can't match it with anything.

"If Sarah was drugged, we'll never know because the most likely drugs had time to metabolize before we were able to get a blood sample.

"The ladies agreed to open their books for us, but there's nothing there. Monthly payments to a variety of charities, expenses, and modest profits split among the partners."

"What about the charities?" Lia asked, relenting and scratching Chewy's head.

"All legit. A number of local rescue charities, all in existence for years, the ASPCA, the Humane Society …. The Doris Day Animal Foundation gets the biggest chunk."

"Those are the folks who are upgrading the park."

"Que Sera, Sera."

"I wish I could help," Lia said.

Peter gave her a stern look. "I'll be much saner if you don't."

"I don't go looking for trouble."

"You don't have to, Babe. Trouble scrawled your number on the bathroom wall. It and all its mullet-headed cousins come looking for you with drool soaking into their boots."

"Not fair, Kentucky Boy. Nobody has tried to kill me lately." Lia's tone was determinedly light.

"No, they've just put you in line to be charged for obstruction of justice and accessory to a crime. And these are your *friends*. I just want you safe."

Lia set down her chopsticks. "I won't be tucked away in a closet, just to make life easier for you. Life isn't about being safe. Life is about dealing with what's in front of you. You and Asia keep telling me this. Do you expect me to turn my back on the people I love?"

"I'd like you to turn your back on this and put it behind you. Get back to your painting. Make another one of those garden things with Bailey. Crochet ear warmers. Anything so I don't have to chase down another freak in the woods before he has a chance to rape you. Please?"

"How am I supposed to put it behind me if it's all around me? If you bring it with you?" Lia flipped the cover of the murder book for emphasis. "You want us to live together. How does that work? Am I just supposed to put my brain on 'Bimbo' when you walk in the door? Are you going to turn the job off when you leave the station? I don't think so."

"God, Lia, I don't want a fight."

"Good. I don't either. But think about what you're asking, and consider how you would feel if I told you all my problems, then expected you to butt out."

"These aren't my problems, they're my job and you aren't a cop. And if you learned how to say 'no' to your friends, you'd get in a lot less trouble."

"Excuse me?"

"You know, if you could say no to people, you might feel comfortable enough with our relationship to stop pushing me away. You just want your little hole where you don't have to deal with anyone, including me. I'm tired of it."

"Wait a minute, Dourson, you just took a left turn here."

"You want to make everyone happy, and you never stop to think about whether people have a right to ask you to put yourself in the situations you've been in."

"Peter, my income comes from doing everything I can to make my clients happy. I like making people happy, and I'm good at it. I like making *you* happy, too. I see no problem with having my own place so I can have some balance."

"Does it ever occur to you, that if you learned to say 'no,' you wouldn't feel compelled to protect yourself by living alone?"

"Where is this coming from?"

"You say you love me, but you don't want us to live together because you don't want to lose yourself. You can't lose yourself if you don't give it away."

"Did your granny stitch that on a sampler, Dourson?" Lia picked up her plate and dumped her dinner in the trash. She set the plate in the sink with the rest of the day's dishes, turning her back to give herself distance. She ran water in the sink, using the activity to settle herself. *Deep breaths, Anderson.*

"Stay or go, whatever you want. But I need time to myself and I'm going into the studio." Lia turned off the tap, abandoning the dishes.

"You can't keep running away, Lia."

"I'm not running away. You just dumped a bunch of stuff all over me and now I need time to think. I'm saying 'no' to continuing this conversation before one of us says something we can't take back."

Lia took her jar of dirty brush water into the kitchen and dumped it in the sink, now clear of dishes. Peter sat at the table, leaning on his elbows with both hands buried in his hair as he examined several color printouts.

Lia walked behind him, laying a hand on his shoulder as she looked down to see what he was so engrossed in.

"Truce?" she asked.

"Is that what you want?" Peter asked without looking up.

"I want you, Peter. I also want to make sure we don't hurt each other in the process of working things out. I'm doing the best I can, but I have to do it in my own way. Can we put this aside for a few days? I promise we'll get back to it."

"You sure?" Peter shoved his chair back.

"Yeah." She brushed the hair off his forehead. "Will you show me what you're looking at?"

Together, the photographs documented the series of bruises that ringed Sarah's throat. The light was different, somehow, revealing distinct impressions of objects. A braided rope. Parts of a large ring. An odd oblong shape made of thin parallel lines.

"These were taken under ultra-violet light? And that's the weapon? This rope?" Lia asked.

"Yeah. It's braided instead of twisted, and it looks like it has a ring on the end. When we saw that, Brent and I figured we had a break. It's not ordinary, and that could focus our investigation. But it's so not ordinary, we don't know what it is."

"And that oblong, what do you think it is?"

"At first we thought it was a footprint, but it's too wide."

"Why would they bother with the rope if they were going to step on her neck? Wouldn't that be enough?"

"You'd think so. No defensive wounds, so she was probably drugged and they had all the time in the world. Whoever did it is strong, because there were no marks on her body or clothing from being dragged. That's a crying shame. If she'd been dragged, we would have some transfer to work with."

"If he carried her, wouldn't you have fiber from his clothes?"

"Crime scene found some blue and green fibers. The color is too bright and cheerful for most men's clothing. Looks like it came from something kids would wear."

"So you're looking for a child who can bench press 200 pounds and likes to play with ponies."

"That about sums it up."

Lia woke in the middle of the night with Peter spooned behind her. She couldn't get the photos of Sarah's neck out of her head. Restless, she left the bed, careful not to disturb Peter. She pulled on a robe and went back into the living room, Honey padding silently after her. The murder book lay open on the coffee table. She paged back until she found the photographs.

She picked up a drawing pad and pencil and swiftly reproduced Sarah's neck and the marks from the murder weapon. Then she stared at her drawing, imagining the form suggested by the marks, joining the curved parts into a D-ring just an inch off the front of Sarah's throat—no, it curved too much to be a D-ring, it had to be round—circling round and round with her pencil to give it weight, defining the gap on one side of the ring that lacked the braid texture, shading the rope to make it appear round.

The gaps in the impression of the ring on Sarah's skin, on one side it would be some smooth material—leather maybe, or plastic—where the rope attached, on the other side, the braid pattern continued inside the circle where the rope slid under the ring and came up through the center.

She imagined the hand pulling the rope through the ring and to the right. Someone would normally hold down the left side that was connected to the ring so they could pull it tighter, but the mark wasn't a handprint.

Instead there were parallel lines. They started at the base of Sarah's throat and leaned left, with the lines perpendicular to an axis about 40 degrees off vertical. The lines were too wide for a shoe, the proportions were wrong. Peter was right about that. Where she could see an edge, it was straight, not curved like a shoe print would be.

Peter said they removed blue and green fibers from the body. She grabbed a case of Prismacolor pencils and gave the rope a candy cane pattern. She chose a dark grey pencil and filled in the odd shape with the parallel lines.

Lia looked at the clock. 3:15 a.m. Drowsy now, she closed her eyes to slits and opened herself to suggestion. When it was 3:22 and no visions were visited upon her, she closed the pad and put it away. She and Honey returned to bed. Peter had rolled onto his other side. She curled up against his back and sent the image to the back of her mind. Something was niggling at her. Pursuing it would chase it away. She would let it simmer as long as it needed. When it boiled over, she would know.

Chapter 17

Thursday, July 14

"I was so angry at Peter last night," Lia told Bailey as they strolled across the park, trailed by dogs.

"Did you tell him?"

"It was obvious. We both backed away from an argument."

"Wouldn't an argument clear the air?" Bailey asked.

"People say that. In my experience, arguments mean people hurt each other more. I'll talk to Peter. I just need some time to think about the things he said first."

"What was the problem?" Bailey asked.

"He doesn't want me involved in Sarah's murder. He wants me to stay in my studio and pretend life is all butterflies and puppies while he goes out and fixes everything. Do you think I'd stay home and expect someone else to deal with it if you were in trouble?"

"I would hope not," Bailey said. "What do you plan to do?"

"Well, I'm not letting him decide for me what I will and won't do. I did that with Rob, and it doesn't work. I promised myself I would never let it happen again."

"And after Rob, you got with Luthor and did whatever you wanted while he went and did Goddess knows what. That wasn't a recipe for paradise, either."

"Bailey, I know, and I'm doing my best to find a middle ground. Still, it would serve Peter right if I solved Sarah's murder. Then I could hold it over his head forever."

"You do realize that's a childish response?" Bailey said.

Lia arched an eyebrow. "Your point is, Ms. Breaking-and-Entering?"

Bailey looked at her. "And look what happened. I'm lucky Peter will still let you play with us."

"See, that's exactly what I mean!"

"Okay, bad choice of words. Terry and I are lucky not to be in jail. We should have stopped at stealing Citrine's curb-side garbage. That was legal. You don't need to compound our mistakes."

"Does that mean you're going to ditch the hacker?"

"Trees is a revolutionary who breaks the law in the service of the higher good and occasionally helps people in need," Bailey proclaimed, her nose at a lofty tilt. "That's different."

"Uh huh. I know better, but I can't help it. Being told not to investigate Sarah's death makes me want to go right out and do it, when I was perfectly happy to leave it alone after that catastrophe with Citrine."

"Everything we've done so far has bombed out. What makes today different?"

"I had an epiphany when I woke up."

"You aren't going to share your epiphany with Peter?"

"Not yet. I want to see what I can do with it first. I need everyone's help."

"More housebreaking?"

"Just brainstorming. Promise. Help me round everyone up."

 ⚘

"I need to pow-wow with everyone," she told the group at the table under the hackberry tree. I had a breakthrough with Sarah's murder. I've narrowed down the pool of suspects—"

"How did you do that?" Steve asked.

"I don't want to say just yet. But we need to focus our attention on Fiber and Snark. I know it's one of the four remaining members. I just don't know how they pulled it off."

"Oh!" Bailey said.

Lia turned to look at her.

"Trees was right! He always said Leroy didn't do it. We should have listened to him."

Lia rolled her eyes, looking for patience.

"And I was right, too, but I didn't know it."

"What are you talking about, Bailey?" Lia asked.

"That tarot card I drew, asking what to do next. The group of three women. We were always supposed to look at a group of women."

"Okay, well, we're doing it now. To get to our problem, none of them were strong enough to carry Sarah up the steps and shove her limp body into the gun barrel. So how was it done?"

"What about the hydraulic lift in the garage?" Terry asked. "Put the body on the lift, lift it up as high as it will go, drag the rolling steps over, drag the body onto the steps and roll it back to the float."

"That wouldn't get the body high enough," Lia said.

"Okay, put the body on the lift, drive a van or SUV over next to the lift, drag the body on top of the SUV, drive the SUV onto the lift, then drag the steps over next to the SUV. Raise the lift so the body is level with the top of the steps and drag the body off the top of the SUV. That should get the body up high enough."

"And re-dress her afterwards? There would have been grime all over her clothes."

"Hmmm," Terry said.

"Something always bothered me about that," Jim said. "If I was shoving a body down a tube, I wouldn't do it feet first."

"Why not?" Bailey asked.

"The knees would buckle and the legs would jam up the tube. If I were doing it, I'd put her in head first, then all the joints flatten out. Her arms were over her head. That added an extra two feet to the space she took up inside the barrel, so she had to be shoved further down the barrel. That makes it twice as hard."

"Yeah, I see what you mean," Jose said.

"Maybe her killer was incompetent," Terry said.

"I think this is important," Lia said. "What do you think, Jim?"

"I don't know yet."

"Okay, anyone else?" Lia asked.

"When I saw her arms hanging out in the parade, I thought it was part of the act," Jose said.

"So did I," Lia said.

"Remember how I told you it would be cool to shoot someone out of the gun?" Jose asked.

"Sure, and I told you to figure out how to do it," Lia said.

"I thought about it, and anyone getting into that gun would climb in feet first. Don't know what that means, though."

"Mon Dieu!" Terry cried, thrusting his index finger in the air. "They did not have to lift her because she climbed in herself!"

"Oh, so the killer says, please oblige me and climb into that float so I can strangle you?" Steve said.

"Of course not," Terry huffed. "There had to be a pretext."

"What pretext can you possibly have for getting someone to climb into a gun barrel?" Steve asked.

"Oh!" Bailey exclaimed.

Everyone turned to look at her.

"Jose wanted to shoot someone out of the gun," Bailey said. "What if Sarah wanted to ride in the barrel during the parade? She could wave at everyone and throw candy."

"So she was trying it out?" Lia said. "But she knew it wasn't designed to hold weight."

"So she does it for fun," Jose said. "Night before the parade, the ladder is there, and she just wants to see what it feels like. She might think it could stand the extra weight for a few minutes."

"But that creates another problem," Lia said. "One of Sarah's bruises suggests the killer stepped on her throat. That had to happen before she got into the gun. If someone stepped on my throat, I wouldn't get up and say,

'Okay, that didn't work. Why don't I climb into that gun barrel and let you finish me off?'"

The group, stumped, sat at the table surrounded by dogs and said nothing.

"The other problem is, why weren't there signs of a struggle?" Lia asked.

Jim cleared his throat. "Someone is with her when she decides to get into the gun barrel. Maybe it was her idea, maybe the killer gave her the idea. She's drunk, maybe unconscious when they killed her. That's why there's no sign she fought back. What do you think?"

"But where did that footprint come from?" Lia asked.

"Are you sure it's a footprint?" Jim asked.

"About 65%."

"The shoe print is a red herring," Terry said. "They did it after they choked her to throw everyone off."

"You're talking about librarians and crime writers," Steve said. "They're researchers at heart. They should know basic forensics. Can you bruise someone if their blood isn't pumping?"

"But she didn't die, not then," Bailey said.

"That was an accident," Steve said. "They thought she was dead when they left her."

"So the funny footprint had to be part of the attack," Jose said.

"Exactly," Steve said.

"Let's stop here. I have enough to think about. If anyone has a brilliant idea, call me."

"What are you going to do now?" Bailey asked.

"She's going to return to the scene of the crime, of course," Terry said. "It's what all detectives do when they're stymied."

⟨✿⟩

"Sure, hang out all you want," Jerry said, getting out from behind his desk. "We're used to having visitors after the cops popped in and out all last week. I finally got my trailer back."

Jerry opened the door that led from the chill of the front office into the bays of the commercial garage. The rolling doors gaped open, vainly hoping to capture a breeze. Sweat pearled on Lia's nose and dripped onto her tee shirt. Heat intensified the smell of grease and motor oil.

Jerry's trailer sat like an empty stage in the car barn. A pair of mechanics had their heads under the hood of a semi parked in the rear of the shop. Lia heard the door close behind her.

Okay Anderson, time for the rubber to hit the road.

Lia sat in one of the ancient folding chairs. She leaned back against the wall, allowing the remnants of the night's chill remaining in the concrete blocks to leech into her shoulders and head.

As she sat, she visualized the giant gun and the way the rolling ladder fit just under the bore. It would be night.

She imagined Sarah, drinking a celebratory glass of wine with someone she trusted. Wine spiked with something secret that would cloud Sarah's judgement and impair her responses faster than the wine would alone.

Jokes are cracked, the next day's triumphal procession imagined, the stress of the last few weeks drops away. Sarah's killer says it's a shame they didn't plan to have someone riding on top of the gun. Sarah says it would be more fun to ride inside the barrel. Her killer eggs her on. "How would you get inside?" Sarah answers, "It would be easy."

Sarah climbs the rolling ladder to prove her point. The bottom of the bore is about 30" above the platform at the top of the ladder. Sarah sits on the platform, then swings her legs up and through the protective rails, into the bore. She then has to twist around so that she is facing the floor and pushing up with her arms, working her thighs, then her hips and torso in, a move she can only do because she is tall and long limbed.

No, wait. Too much work.

Sarah carries a folding chair up the ladder and places it in front of the gun bore. She sits in the chair, folding her legs so her knees are under her chin, then extends her feet forward, sliding them into the gun barrel. Then it's easy-peasy to push up with her hands on the seat and slide her hips in. Then she turns over.

Her faceless killer, laughing and cheering, climbs the steps up to the platform. She brings the wine and the glasses with her, and her purse. Strange, bringing her purse, but there is something in it she needs. She sits on the chair and they talk, refilling Sarah's glass when it empties.

Sarah becomes drowsy while her killer watches for the perfect moment. Does she feel tension as she approaches the moment for action? Does she consider backing out? What drives her? Is it greed or hatred? Is it elation? Does she drop her mask in those last moments and let the rage show, the rage that must be under everything for her to murder her friend? Or is she smug?

The killer opens her purse and removes the rope with the loop in the end. She has drugged Sarah and she has this odd garrote. She knows she is not strong enough to strangle Sarah with her hands, but she saw the rope and the idea grew that she could use it to do this thing.

Now she is here and she has the noose in her hands and she widens it, and Sarah does not realize anything is happening until her killer lifts the noose to slip it over her head. Sarah slaps at the rope, flailing her arms, but too drunk to fully grasp the danger.

The noose is silly, an annoyance. Sarah does not want to play her friend's peculiar game. Perhaps she is laughing. She flaps her arms too weakly to scratch or bruise. Eventually she tires, and the noose falls neatly over her head.

Sarah's killer pulls the noose as tight as she can, but it is not enough. Sarah begins to cough and twist her head about. With Sarah facing down, her killer positions herself under Sarah, applying force upwards. It takes a long time to strangle someone. Her arms tire and fail. Sarah is not dead.

The killer falls back on the platform, exhausted. She needs leverage. How will she get enough leverage? There is no backing out, no way that Sarah will mistake the bruises forming around her neck as anything but what they are.

Her killer climbs down and searches the garage. Perhaps she could find some tool to hit Sarah with? But the tools are locked up and she does not want blood to reveal Sarah's presence inside the float.

Sarah's killer thinks about lying on the metal platform, her arms exhausted and unable to complete the task. She thinks about the failure of her plans, of orange jumpsuits and ugly, brutal women.

And then Lia understands.

What am I doing?

Lia looked over the group assembled in the living room at SCOOP. Peter and Brent were there, along with Leroy and Linda and the ladies of Fiber and Snark. Bailey refused to be left out, saying her role was to provide moral support. Lia looked at Bailey, who winked back.

Debby sat closest to the foyer. Alice and Cecilie shared the sofa by the kitchen with Leroy and Linda. Carol sat with her sprained foot propped on an ottoman next to the den, where the kitties were penned out of consideration for those who were not feline fanatics. More than thirty cats of all ages and sizes milled behind the pet gate, mewing for the rolling bin of kibble sitting at Carol's feet. Peter, Brent and Bailey shared the sofa on Lia's right.

A huge tom batted at the pet gate, making it wobble.

"Can someone shove the kibble bin out of sight?" Debby asked. "The noise is going to make me crazy."

Bailey jumped up and moved the bin past Carol's chair.

"Just tuck it beside me," Carol said. "That will be far enough."

When the cats settled, Lia cleared her throat. "I guess you're wondering why I asked everyone to meet me here." She paused. "There have been further developments."

She took a moment to observe faces. The ladies looked baffled. Leroy narrowed his eyes. Linda leaned forward with avid interest. Peter frowned.

"Well?" Cecilie asked.

"Cecilie, do you mind if I get into the donations closet? There's something I need to show everyone."

Cecilie waved a hand. "Be my guest."

Lia donned a pair of neoprene gloves before she disappeared into the closet. She reappeared with an armload of leashes and lay them in the middle of the floor.

Lia handed Peter a pair of gloves and pointed to a colorful length of braided rope peeking out from the bottom of the pile.

"The blue and green one. Take a look at it."

Peter withdrew the leash. It ended, not with the usual clip, but in a loop created by feeding the leash through a brass ring that had been joined to the end with a folded piece of leather.

"That's a slip lead. It's generally used with show dogs. Renee has one for Dakini, but that one is rolled leather. I saw this in the closet 2 weeks ago."

"If you want the damn leash, just take it," Debby groused. "I don't know why you needed the peanut gallery to raid the donation closet."

"I don't want it, but I think Peter might. Would that work, Peter?"

"Something like this might." Lia expected him to examine the leash. Instead he searched the faces surrounding them.

"We don't want to hear about your kinky sex lives. Seriously, Lia—"

"I do believe this is about murder, not sex, Mrs. Carrico," Brent said softly. "I believe we are looking at the weapon used to strangle Sarah Schellenger. Do you have any other surprises for us, Lia?"

Lia looked at Peter. "I might. May I proceed?"

Peter waved his hand in the universal "please do" gesture.

"Okay." Lia took a deep breath. "I know we all want to know the truth about Sarah. Well, everybody but one person, anyway.

"By chance I saw ultra-violet photographs the coroner's office took of Sarah's neck. They revealed the shape and texture of the object used to strangle Sarah. Then I remembered seeing a leash here that might have created most of the bruises."

"There must be hundreds of slip leads in Cincinnati," Alice said. I think there are a couple more in that pile. Why do you think it's this one?"

"Peter?" Lia asked.

"Fibers. We collected fibers from Sarah's clothes that are likely to match this leash."

"Wouldn't the fibers be on Sarah's neck if that was used to strangle her?" Alice asked.

"There probably were fibers embedded in her neck, but any trace evidence was lost when Sarah was prepped for surgery."

"You honestly think one of us did it? We loved Sarah," Cecilie said.

"Whoever did this had intimate knowledge of everyone here," Lia said. "They knew Alice kept her cell phone in her purse and never answered it at night. They knew Carol was going to Clifton to pick up baba ganooj, and that she liked to take the alley shortcut to the parking lot."

"That was Leroy," Carol insisted.

Leroy leaned forward to respond, but held back when Linda placed a hand on his arm.

"No. Someone wanted everyone to think it was Leroy, just like they wanted Alice to think Leroy left her a message, and that she erased it by accident. The message was a tape spliced out of recordings. The killer called when no one would answer the phone because they had no way to fake conversation.

Our killer knew that Cecilie swims at Twin Towers every morning and keeps her water bottle in her unlocked car. And they knew Leroy could never resist a woman who looked like Kat Dennings."

Cecilie turned to Alice. "Who's Kat Dennings?"

Alice shushed her.

"All that intimate knowledge pointed directly at you four." Lia gestured, indicating the ladies of Fiber and Snark. "The big problem has always been that the person who killed Sarah also lifted her into the gun barrel without collecting the kind of trace evidence that would show if she had been dragged. It pointed to someone who was powerful enough to lift 150 pounds of dead weight and carry it more than a dozen feet. But none of you have that kind of strength.

"I called upon my panel of consultants." Lia nodded at Bailey, who beamed. "After much deliberation, we realized Sarah climbed into the gun barrel—"

"What in Heaven's name would make her do an idiot thing like that?" Debby said.

"After two glasses of wine, all it would take is a suggestion that it would be fun to ride in the barrel during the parade. Who wouldn't want to try it out?" Alice said. "I thought about it. I imagine Sarah did, as well."

Lia caught surprised looks passing between Peter and Brent. She hoped they were watching the crowd, because she kept forgetting.

"Half of us still aren't strong enough to strangle someone, even if we conned them into disposing of their own body," Cecilie said.

"Wait a minute, you think it was me or Alice?" Debby said.

"Not so fast," Lia said. "I went back to the garage and tried to replay the scene in my head. Once Sarah was in the gun barrel, she drank more wine or was drugged. Then it would have been easy to strangle her without resistance. But to strangle someone, you have to continue the chokehold for several minutes.

"In addition to the impression of the slip lead on Sarah's throat, there was a series of parallel lines forming a shape covering the left half of Sarah's throat. The lines were in the spot where you would apply pressure with one hand while pulling the end of the leash with the other. I thought they could have been shoe tread, except the shape was too wide and the side was straight instead of curved.

"Did you know that the strongest muscles in a woman's body are in the legs? The pattern of the bruises suggest that someone stepped on her neck while killing her. But, what if they put the loop around Sarah's neck, sat in one of the folding chairs and braced one foot against her neck, shoving Sarah's head and neck against the the inside top of the tube? The noose would be pinned in place with one foot while they pulled the leash with both hands. The position would still be fatiguing, which may have led to the killer releasing the hold before Sarah was dead."

"It's an interesting theory," Alice said, "but it doesn't prove it was any of us, even if you find Sarah's DNA on that leash. She could have handled that leash any time. None of us have a motive."

The cats in the next room resumed yowling for their dinner.

"If that's all you have, we have cats to feed," Debby said, rising from her chair.

"There's more," Lia said. "The footprint on Sarah's neck was so odd, the coroner wasn't convinced it was a shoe. Along with the blocky shape, it had a sole that was rounded on the bottom from front to back. Just like the boot Carol wore over her sprained ankle before she switched out to the lighter splint she's wearing now."

"That's outrageous!" Carol bolted upright in her chair. "My ankle still hasn't healed. I just resumed driving yesterday. I couldn't even get to Jerry's garage on my own, much less apply enough pressure to choke Sarah to death!

"Besides, I dropped the boot off at Saint Vincent de Paul with several boxes of old clothes the week before Sarah died."

"Really? You were in an awful hurry to get rid of it. What if your foot took a turn for the worse?" Lia asked.

"Could someone have bought or stolen Carol's boot?" asked Alice.

"There was a lot of money involved in arranging Leroy's kidnapping, but you didn't expect anyone to find that out, did you, Carol?" She turned to the group. "Who is in a better position than an accountant to siphon off funds?"

"The books were examined. They're clean," Debby insisted.

"You keep forgetting Carol's sprain," Cecilie said.

"There was no sprain," Lia said.

Carol slapped the arm of her chair. "What are you talking about? You took me to the hospital! You saw my ankle! It was twice its size."

"A neatly manufactured illusion. Once you became my prime suspect, I tried to research ways to fake a sprain that would pass with a doctor, and had no luck. Then I called Steve at the Homeless Association and asked him to poll some of his clients. Many of them have been in jail. No one is more creative than a prisoner in getting out of work details."

"What did you find?" Peter asked.

"Inject 20 ccs of saline near the joint, and it will swell up immediately and last long enough to be seen by a doctor. Grab one of those broken half-bricks by the parking lot, hit yourself on the forehead and scrape yourself up a bit and it looks like you've had a bad fall.

"Your leg has been fine all along. You faked the sprain on your right ankle so you could pretend you were stuck at home because you couldn't drive. No one would suspect you were behind everything that happened."

"I can't believe you'd accuse me of such a thing," Carol sputtered.

"Where's the proof, Lia?" Peter asked.

Lia withdrew a paper bag from her purse and held it in front of Carol. "It's in here.

"I remembered seeing several hypodermic needles in the weeds when I picked up your things that night. When Steve told me how you could have faked your injury, I knew you would have done it on the spot. You'd want witnesses at the restauraunt who could say your leg was fine before you headed for the parking lot.

"You injected yourself and tossed the syringes you used into the weeds. You left them in place because you did not want to be seen picking them up later. I went back down today and they were still there."

Lia opened the bag and removed several used, weathered syringes and laid them on a side table.

"What do you want to bet at least one of them has Carol's fingerprints and traces of saline?"

Carol leapt out of her chair, grabbing the bin of kibble and dumping it in the middle of the room. She yanked the pet gate, already loose, free from the doorway and tossed it down. The unleashed horde of famished cats poured into the room.

Carol dodged around the side of the melee, toppling cat trees and sending felines flying and clawing through the air. More cats jumped from the catwalks, eliciting shrieks as they landed on heads and in laps. Several collided with would-be pursuers. Debby repelled an airborne tabby attempting to claw her way to the safety of Debby's shoulder, tossing it on Alice, who fell against Brent, who cursed as he tried to keep his balance and stop Alice from falling. He failed, toppling with Alice to the floor. They nearly disappeared under the tide of yowling, brawling cats converging on the mound of kibble.

Beyond the uproar, Carol ducked out the patio door.

Blocked by roiling felines, Peter ran out the front door and around the house. He met up with Brent and Leroy at the back alley. Brent's arms were clawed and he was covered with fur.

"She must have parked back here," Brent said. "I have no idea which way she went."

"Damn. For a little old lady, she sure is fast," Leroy said. "Are you going after her? I want to come."

Peter and Brent looked at each other. Just as Peter was about to blurt out the standard, "No civilians," Brent said, "Someone needs to take care of the ladies."

Peter and Brent ran around the house to the Explorer and hopped in. Brent called in a BOLO on Carol's car while Peter tore around the block in a desperate attempt to head Carol off.

"Watch those corners," Brent said. "Your flying detritus is going to stain my suit." He picked up the sticky wrapper from a blueberry Pop Tart and shoved it into a crumpled paper bag lying in the footwell.

"It's already got blood and cat hair on it."

"That's no reason to abuse it further."

Peter rounded another corner on two wheels, taking him onto Spring Grove Avenue and directly into a construction zone.

"Damn." He slammed the heel of his palm against the steering wheel.

"We could cut through the cemetery," Brent suggested, nodding to the historic burial ground on their left.

"That's a maze. We'll get to the intersection faster if we just hold tight."

Peter's radio crackled with chatter, but none of it was about Carol.

They crawled to the light and turned onto Winton Road. Peter stomped on the gas, racing up the empty lane to a long hill.

"Where are we going?" Brent asked. "Don't you think she's headed for the airport?"

"She had enough of a jump on us that she would have made the highway already, if that's where she was going. If it isn't, I might be able to cut her off at Cross County and Hamilton."

"Ah. I like knowing there's logic in play. Here I thought you were tearing up your transmission for no good reason."

Thirty minutes later, Peter and Brent returned to SCOOP to find nervous cats prowling behind the repaired pet gate. Bailey was a cheerful anomaly, scooping out litter pans while the shell-shocked ladies of Fiber and Snark picked kibble out of the carpet. Leroy and Linda huddled over her phone. *Internet research? Facebook BOLOs?* Lia sat alone on a sofa, head in her hands.

Peter sat down beside her, wrapping one arm around her shoulders and pulling her against him so that her head rested on his chest.

"I made a mess of things, didn't I?" She mumbled.

"You revealed confidential information from our investigation, possibly endangering any case we choose to make later; you confronted a killer outside of a controlled environment and without a plan to contain her; our killer is in the wind, and who knows how many man-hours it's going to take to catch her. Please, please, tell me those syringes are not from the Clifton Merchant's lot. I don't want to add tampering with evidence to the list."

Lia shook her head without looking at him. "Someone cleaned up all the trash. Steve knows where you can find discarded syringes. He got them for me."

"Why didn't you come to me with this?"

"I felt hurt and discounted last night. I wanted to make a point, and the point I wound up making is that I have no business messing with your cases."

Peter used an index finger to skim the hair out of her eyes. Their green shimmered up at him and reminded him of the first time he'd seen her. Then she'd been a traumatized witness. She was wounded today, too, but he wasn't sure he knew everything he'd done to cause the wound.

"You were brilliant," he offered.

"Peter, I screwed up. She got away."

"You figured it out. We could have done without the theatrics, but you identified the murder weapon, and discovered how Carol faked her sprain. You built a case."

"A case with no proof. I thought if she were pressured in front of everyone, she would crack."

"She did, just not in the way you expected. I wish you had turned everything over to us. We would have taken a second look at those accounts, gotten a warrant for the boot and the leash, and sweated her out in interview."

"Why didn't you stop me? You had to know what I was doing."

Peter rubbed his temple. "I—uh—figured you'd fall on your face and make my point for me."

"You got that right."

"Not exactly. I haven't been giving you enough credit, and I'm sorry."

"Peter, it's my fault she got away."

"On the bright side, I was invited to the party this time, and for once no one was trying to kill you. Don't worry about Carol. I don't think she'll get too far."

Brent approached, followed by Alice, Cecilie and Debby.

"That was impressive. What do you do for an encore, Lia?" Debby asked.

Lia's face remained impassive, but Peter knew she took the hit.

"Don't shoot the messenger, now," Brent said.

"All this time it's been Carol. She's known Sarah since they were children. I can't believe she'd do such a thing," Alice said.

"Then why did she run?" Cecilie said.

"Oh, I get that she did it. I just can't believe she did it. I wish I knew why."

"Ladies," Peter said, "I know you're in shock, but we have more important things to do. Right now, we have to figure out where she's going."

"How are we supposed to know what she's thinking?" Cecilie asked. "We've obviously been clueless for years."

"Who else would know how her mind works better than you?" Lia said. "She mentioned making suggestions for the books. Maybe you could start there."

"More like, how Carol's mind doesn't work," Debby said. "We had to keep a tight leash on her, she always wanted to jump the shark."

"Jump the shark?" Brent frowned.

"A fatal case of going overboard."

"What would her contingency plan be?" Brent asked.

"She doesn't have time for plastic surgery," Debby said. "I assume you've notified all the airports within two hundred miles?"

"She talked about bug-out bags, having everything you need to get out of the country stashed where she could get to it." Alice said.

"Bus station locker?" Bailey suggested.

"Those lockers are on timers now," Cecilie said. You can't leave anything in them over 24 hours."

"A coat check?" offered Steve.

"Too risky," Debby said. "In *Day of the Saguaro*, Koi used a hotel luggage check to hide cash, fake papers, bank account numbers and the key to a car registered in her new identity that was parked in a public garage nearby. In the book, the bellman accidentally gives the bag to someone who owned an identical bag."

"She'll know you've already notified the airports," Cecilie said.

"If she's renting a spot in a garage, why wouldn't she keep everything in her car?" Lia asked. "She could hide it easily enough."

"Too easy," Alice said. "I'm not sure where she's going, but I bet she'll have a white wig. She said the best way to disguise yourself is to look older, because no woman in her right mind would do that."

"Where would she keep a car?" Peter asked.

"Storage unit!" Cecilie said, jumping up as if she meant to run out the door to catch Carol that very moment.

"The closest is on Spring Grove Avenue, just above Mitchell. It's your best bet." Debby said.

"Spring Lawn, behind the cemetery is closer." Alice said.

"It will have a combination lock," Cecilie added.

"Brent, with me," Peter said. "Look up all the storage places within 5 miles and update the BOLO while I drive."

"Any luck?" Lia asked when Peter dragged himself in three hours later.

He half-sat, half-fell onto Lia's sofa. Viola jumped up beside him, sneering at Lia when she handed Peter a beer. He took a long swallow and exhaled noisily.

"We checked security tapes at the most likely storage units. Her car doesn't show up."

Lia folded her arms and looked away. "I'm so sorry. I really hoped you would find her."

"Let's not talk about it. Right now, I want to get back to the evening I thought I was going to have before my girlfriend went off the rails."

"Peter, I—"

"Shhhh. Let it go. It happened. My brain is too fried to think about it right now. Come over here and help me feel human for a while."

Chapter 18

It had worked. Elation threatened to bubble up like champagne frothing out of the bottle. Carol fought with a smile, which resulted in a sort of twitch. She fought it down as she closed her eyes and sank into her seat on the train.

She felt a light touch on her arm.

"More coffee, Mrs. Ashling?"

"Thank you, no." Carol handed her cup to the attendant. She leaned back and shut her eyes. "I think I'll take a nap now. It's been a very busy morning."

The moment Lia brought the leashes out, Carol began plotting her escape from SCOOP, hoping it wasn't necessary. After all, many people had access to that closet. She'd still expected to walk out of the meeting. Lia had seen her sprained ankle and taken her to hospital. Who knew she'd suspect it was faked?

Thank heavens she'd spent an hour a day on her treadmill while she was supposedly disabled. It was that initial sprint that enabled her to get to her car before Leroy and Dourson could fight their way through the cats. By the time they were in pursuit, she was halfway to the rented garage where her contingency plan waited.

The worst moment had been stopping for gas on her way out of Cincinnati. Careless of Sarah, to drive around with the needle in the red. Nerves prickled Carol's skin all over, as if she were standing naked in the the middle of a football stadium filled to capacity. Surely everyone was watching her?

But why would they? She'd camouflaged Sarah's car by removing the cat lady car magnets and covering the bumper stickers with such sentiments as "God, Guns and Guts Made America Great." The plates were those of a bedridden client. The switch would probably not be discovered until the woman died.

She left Cincinnati wearing a white wig in an old fashioned style that softened her face. To further the impression of great age, she'd created a slight dowager's hump by sewing a pad in her summer-weight blazer. Eyebrow pencil deepened the wrinkles on her face, which was then then dusted with enough loose power to make anyone who came within three feet of her sneeze.

Carol beamed at the cashier despite her paranoia, handing over two twenty dollar bills, brushing the girl's hand in the process. The cashier stretched her lips in a perfunctory smile and moved her gaze to the next customer in line. She did not suspect she'd just been touched by a murderer.

Her disguise appeared foolproof. Still, every police car she saw sent her heart rate into the red zone. She did not relax until she was north of Dayton.

Planning was everything, especially when it was based on good research. Few people knew that Port Huron, a town north of Detroit, was a haven for smugglers during prohibition. Kegs of Canadian liquor were ferried with impunity across the Saint Clair River, the journey embarked upon in the middle of night at the waterway's darkest and narrowest point.

It was a matter of math. Most people would not realize it was quicker to drive to Canada than it was to get on an international flight in Cincinnati. While the police were watching the local airports, She was driving north in Sarah's car, each mile taking her further from pursuit and capture.

Carol pulled over at the Love's Travel Stop outside Toledo because she did not want to arrive at Port Huron too early. Arby's was the only place to eat, so she'd dawdled over her farmer salad as long as she could and went up to the counter a second time for onion rings. She shouldn't eat fried foods, but Arby's made such wonderful onion rings. Afterwards, the chocolate turnover called her name. She denied herself. Someone might remember her if she made three trips to the counter. She did not want to be remembered.

A trip to the ladies room allowed her to swap her old-lady guise for Teva sport sandals, quick-dry shorts, and a head wrap. She bought a smartphone at the Love's store, filled her gas tank halfway—she wouldn't need more—then spent an hour in her car registering the phone and downloading apps.

With the alarm on her new phone set for eleven-thirty, she reclined the driver's seat as far as it would go and closed her eyes.

Carol drained the last of a cup of ghastly coffee as she drove into the south end of Port Huron. She hoped it would not give her heartburn.

A factory sat across the Busha Highway from the Saint Clair river. Carol parked Sarah's car in the employee lot, knowing that with the factory running twenty four hours, the car would not be discovered for weeks. A fold-up luggage trolly provided the means to haul a light-weight inflatable boat, a trolling motor, and her carry-on to a little-used landing she'd discovered on Google Earth.

Practice inside her storage unit enabled her to inflate the boat in the dark. Wading into the impenetrable black of the river gave her a bad moment, as did climbing into the wobbly boat. She shoved off with an oar and turned on the trolling motor. The boat ran aground at the Sarnia Indian Reserve fifteen not very strenuous minutes later.

She left the boat behind. The next fisherman to arrive was sure to tuck it away in the trunk of his car. After all, it cost five hundred dollars and was almost new.

Carol cut through the strip of houses along the Canadian shore, into the woods at the heart of the reserve and found a soft place under a tree to rest. She patted her pocket to ensure her pepper spray was still there, then lay her head on her carryon and drifted into restless sleep.

Sunlight and twittering birds roused Carol earlier than she would have liked. Her joints ached. She cursed herself for not bringing something warm for her one night in the Canadian woods. She stood up one cracking joint at a time and decided that would likely be the most difficult thing she would do all day.

She did what she could to brush the bits of twigs and grass off her clothes, then set out on the four mile walk to the Sarnia train station. It could not be helped. Sarnia bus service did not extend this far south. By the time she reached a Tim Hortons doughnut shop, she was ready to cry.

⚘

Carol roused from her nap on the train and used her new phone to pull up the Toronto-Pearson International Airport schedule on her browser. She booked herself a first class seat on an afternoon flight to Cozumel. Running north, only to fly south. The route was, at first glance, irrational. All the better to confound pursuers.

The Toronto airport had a large number of international flights daily, with Cancun and Cozumel serving as her gateway to Central America. She hadn't decided between Belize and Costa Rica as her new home. Unheard of for her to not have every last detail nailed down. She would have fun traveling around before she settled. The thought of being so spontaneous made her dizzy.

⚘

Carol steadied herself with one hand on the long, stainless steel table at the airport security checkpoint while she used the other to remove her shoes. She lined them up precisely in the bin, setting her purse next to them, then her sweater. The nice young man in front of her lifted her carryon onto the rollers that fed into the scanner.

Daphne Ashling's passport and identification passed muster. Once she was through the metal detector, she would be safe. The measures that kept terrorists out would protect her her from pursuers.

253

She smiled brilliantly at the man monitoring the metal detector. He waved her through, then nodded politely as she crossed from danger into freedom.

"Enjoy your journey," he said.

"I certainly will," she answered.

Belongings retrieved, she strolled, lifting her head to take in the sun streaming through the skylights running the length of the terminal. There was time for a lovely, leisurely meal before she boarded.

She stopped to scan a map of the terminal, trying to decide what she was in the mood to eat. Indian and Thai were too spicy and sushi too adventurous for her, but the panini bar sounded promising.

Carol had just placed her order on the table's iPad when she felt a hard hug from behind.

"Auntie! I can't believe you're here."

Carol jerked away and turned to face a pair of smiling red lips and gray eyes.

"Don't say a word." The whispered command came from Carol's other side as a restraining hand landed on her shoulder.

Linda Lyle slipped into the chair next to Carol's and leaned forward.

"This is so amazing, running into you like this" Linda enthused.

Carol felt two sharp points against her bare thigh.

"Now, don't scream, Auntie," Linda said, her voice lower, "I have a taser pressed against your leg. If you make one move, I will juice you up and claim you had a seizure."

"You're bluffing," Carol sneered. "You can't bring a taser through airport security."

"You'd be surprised, *Auntie*," Leroy said, taking the seat on Carol's other side. "You can't bring a taser, but you can bring everything you need to make one."

Leroy placed a disposable camera on the table, keeping his hand on it. Two screws jutted out of the end closest to Carol. She frowned at the device.

"The screws are wired to the battery in the camera. Linda was kind enough to make one for me, too. There's no way to control the power level." Leroy leaned over so he could whisper. "That means you can't predict what will happen when you use it. Makes things more fun, don't you think?" He sat back up. "Now, we're going to talk."

"I think I'm hungry," Linda said. "I see no reason why we can't have a civilized meal while we're here."

"How did you find me?" Carol asked.

"Wasn't hard," Leroy grinned the infectious and disarming grin that sold so many books. "I remember an argument you had with the others over the best way to slip out of the country for one of the books. It was on that god-awful boring drive to Chicago for a book signing. No one ever gives me credit for paying attention. You were outvoted because your plan was too complicated. I thought it was brilliant.

"When you poofed yesterday, I knew exactly what you'd do. I figured airport security was the one sure place we could head you off, if we could get here before you. Linda was nice enough to offer me a ride. I imagine we passed you on the road."

"What do you want?" Carol gritted out between her teeth.

"Auntie, don't sulk," Linda cajoled. "We're having a reunion. You should be happy."

Linda tapped on the table's iPad and pulled up the menu. "Leroy, what are you in the mood for? I think I'm going for the baked penne. Easier to eat with one hand."

"I'll take the roast beef panini and a beer. Tell me, *Auntie*, how much did you sock away in the Caymans?"

Carol glared.

"Ooh, she's giving you the stink-eye," Linda said. "Honey, we just want you to take a minute and think about what's at stake."

They paused their conversation as the food arrived.

"All those foreign editions and audiobooks. So many income streams that never made it into the Bang Bang Books account," Leroy said, watching the waiter leave. "I had no idea I was so popular."

"Do the others know?" Carol asked.

"Not yet. How much is there? Two million? Three? You know you can't spend it all. I want my share."

"And you'll let me board my plane?"

"First we need to take care of business. We'll need you on hand until the transfers are completed. That might be tomorrow."

"I'm not leaving this terminal," Carol said.

"Now, Auntie," Linda said, forking up a bite of penne. "Umm, this is so good. I'd give you a bite, but you might spit it back at me. You're going to get sick and Leroy will get a wheelchair so we can roll you out of here. That's if you cooperate. If we have to, we'll bash you on the head and strap you in."

"I bet she has everything stored on her phone," Leroy said. "We could just take it and let her go."

"You wouldn't be able to crack it," Carol sneered.

"You hired a hacker to look for me. I'm sure I can pay him more than you did."

"Oh, dear," Linda sighed. "I was so hoping we could be civilized about this."

"I feel ill," Carol said.

"That's the spirit," Leroy said.

Chapter 19

Saturday, July 17

Peter eyed Carol Cohn on the monitor outside the downtown interrogation room. She sat at rigid attention that could only have been learned at the hands of nuns during her childhood. Her expression, one of superiority, gave no ground. On the other hand, her quick-dry shorts and wrinkle-proof knit top had been defeated through many hours of riding chained-up in Linda's RV. The formerly perfect pouf of red hair hung in tatters around her face.

Not feeling any remorse, are you?

"Some killer, huh?" Brent said, nodding at the small figure. "Shall we go shake a confession out of her?"

Brent followed Peter into the interview room. They stood before her, arms crossed.

Carol looked up with a quizzical expression. "I don't understand why I'm here."

"I imagine it's for the same reason you toppled three cat trees and ran out of Cecilie Watkins' house."

"Those cat trees have always been wobbly. They must have fallen on their own."

"Dumping Sarah's car in Port Huron? Sneaking into Canada? Flying under a fake passport?"

"Research." Carol gave her mouth a tiny, smug quirk.

"You've been very busy," Brent said, sighing with a sorrowful look. "Funneling automatic deposits from your book vendors through an account you opened using the social security number of a deceased client, then shooting the works into the Caymans."

Carol shrugged. "A girl has to have a hobby."

"And Sarah Schellenger? Is strangling your friends another one of your hobbies?" Brent asked.

Carol looked at them and blinked once, slowly, like a lizard. Her glasses magnified her eyes, reinforcing the resemblance.

"What happened with Sarah?" Peter asked. "You were lifelong friends."

"Not friends. Not exactly."

"No?" Brent asked.

Peter and Brent remained still, waiting for Carol to fill the silence. Finally she closed her eyes and heaved a sigh.

"Did you really grill Leroy for six hours when he returned?" Carol asked.

"That we did," Brent said. "But I'm sure that's nothing to a woman who rowed across the Saint Clair River in pitch darkness."

"Speaking of Leroy," Peter said, "did he tell you he recorded your conversation in the RV? The one where you accessed your offshore bank account? The shot of your balance has great resolution."

Carol pursed her lips, thinking. Brent and Peter waited. Peter imagined she was doing the math: eventually she would tell them, if it took six hours or ten hours, or twenty. With the bank accounts, they had too much evidence for her to bluff her way out. Finally she shook her head and scoffed quietly. "I always knew he'd be trouble.

"There's always this one person," Carol continued, "They're younger, taller, prettier, smarter. Everyone likes them. If you bring cupcakes you baked yourself to the church potluck, nobody eats them because they're too busy stuffing themselves with her Oreos. If you go to a party together, all the men ignore you while they try to get her attention. She marries a man who adores her. It doesn't matter what you do, she always does it better and her life is always easier.

"I suggest an idea for the books, and everyone poo-poos it. Sarah suggests the exact same thing two days later and they're all on board, because she's so brilliant. Why is that?"

"You resented Sarah," Brent said. "You felt unappreciated. Is that why you embezzled from the group?"

"It was too easy," she smirked. "They left all the paperwork to me. 'Go back to your adding machine, Carol,'" she mimicked. "'We're the creative folks. We need you to pick up after us and keep us out of trouble with the IRS. We don't need you for the fun stuff.'"

"If you hated her so much, why did you belong to Fiber and Snark?" Brent asked.

"I didn't hate her, not exactly. I was her—the young girls call it a 'frenemy'. The group was fun when it started. Sarah was just an irritant, like a little rock in your shoe that you can't ever shake out, and every once in a while it gets into the right spot and it stabs your foot. Most of the time it was fine."

"What changed, Mrs. Cohn?"

"When Frank passed, I had to find ways to fill my time. That's when I started going to Sarah's group. Anything to get out of that house. Then the writing started, and that was exciting, making money with the books. But Sarah decided we needed to give it all away, and everyone just nods their heads like a bunch of puppets."

"So you made sure you got your share. Did Sarah realize what was going on?" Peter asked.

"Of course not. Nobody was minding the store but me."

"Why kill her?" Peter asked.

"It was the house."

"What house?" Brent asked, perplexed.

"Mrs. Peltier's house? The one Sarah bought, next to Alma's?" Peter asked.

"I loved that house since I was a little girl. That was before Ruth went dotty and turned it into a warehouse for the Home Shopping Network. I'd walk past it on the way to school and pretend I lived there. I picked a room for myself, one with a turret, and I imagined myself sitting on the window seat and waving at the world from my castle.

"Ruth never liked me. I never once got to go inside. I was in high school when Sarah started first grade, and my mother expected me to walk Sarah home every day. Ruth invited *her* in for cookies every Thursday.

"I'd be walking alongside Sarah, and Ruth would open her door and call out to Sarah and ask her in for a snack. The next day, Sarah would jabber on about the cookies and how many she ate, and she'd show me some gaudy piece of costume jewelry Ruth gave her to play with.

"I never should have told Sarah the house was on the market. She didn't bother to think about me. She just barged in and outbid everyone. One person shouldn't have so much."

"She killed Sarah over the *house*?" Debby was astounded.

"She knew the contract would be voided if Sarah died before the closing," Lia explained. "That would give her another chance at it. But I think the house was just the final straw after a lifetime of envying everything Sarah had."

"What about Leroy? Why did she drag him into it?" Debby asked.

"Leroy's kidnapping had nothing to do with Sarah. He'd made noises to Carol about getting involved in writing the books and running the business. Carol knew if he got his hands on the spreadsheets, he would figure out what she was doing. The accounting was perfect according to the deposits that were made to your bank, but the foreign editions were published under a separate account and the royalties were deposited into Carol's offshore bank.

"When Carol decided to kill Sarah, Leroy's disappearance made him a convenient scapegoat. She faked the phone call to Alice by splicing together recordings of practice interviews she did with Leroy, which she manipulated to get the phrases she needed. Then she added in enough static to make it sound like a bad connection, and when Alice's back was turned, she deleted Alice's messages so it could never be analyzed.

"She faked the attack on herself and drugged Cecilie's sport drink, so when Sarah died, it would point back to Leroy and everyone would think it was about the books. If the only attack was on Sarah, the police would look at other motives for her death.

"Carol carried the burner phone with her and put the battery in when she wanted it to ping and place Leroy nearby."

"That little—" Debby's face was now red.

"I think the word you're looking for is 'biotch,'" Alice said.

"Why did she get him out of the way in the first place? What good was that going to do? He was still going to come back," Cecilie said.

"The way I understand it, it was a two-pronged plan. By forcing him to write all day long for a month, she expected him to develop such an aversion to writing that he would happily return to being your handsome but clueless frontman," Lia said.

"But if he didn't?" Cecilie asked.

"The disappearance of Lucas Cross shortly before his next release was bound to send sales into the stratosphere. She figured she might need to cut her losses and run. She was hoping to get a big score before that was necessary," Lia concluded.

"Poor Leroy," Alice said.

"Poor Leroy, hah!" Debby said. "He ran off with that hussy."

"Citrine?" Alice asked, mouth gaping.

"No, the one that kidnapped him. They made that little side trip to Toronto so they could give us Carol as their going away present."

"No!" The other women said in unison.

"Carol's plan backfired," Debby continued. "He says he got his rhythm after the first week of being chained to a laptop and has decided he's a writer.

"Remember Nick Russell from AustinCon? Leroy and what's-her-face headed off in her RV to meet up with Nick and his wife in Minnesota. Nick has promised to mentor him while they travel around the country."

"But our launch!" Cecilie wailed.

"He said it was time we stood up to take our bows, and the notoriety will carry us through until our fans get used to us."

"I don't know if there can be an us without Sarah," Cecilie mumbled.

"Maybe we need to reinvent ourselves. I miss my quirky villagers. I'd like to get back to that series," Alice said.

"I'm tired of that Koi bitch," Debby said to Cecilie. "What say you and I kill her off in a spectacular way."

"We could toss in Colt for a twofer," Cecilie said. "They meet, fall in love, and get blown to bits on the honeymoon."

"Now you're talking."

Epilogue

Saturday, August 6

It was the voices outside that woke Peter. That and slamming car doors. This would have to be the Saturday of the damn community garage sale.

He'd had too much paperwork to catch up on the night before, and slept through his usual Saturday morning at the dog park with Lia. The sun was high and laser hot where it shot through the crack between the curtains, hitting him between the shoulders. He started to pull the pillow over his head, but Viola nosed in next to him, frantically licking his face with an "uh, uh, uh."

Dog. Walk. Right. A pair of shorts hanging from a doorknob were handy and still wearable. He grabbed a tee shirt, pulling it over his head on the way out while Viola whimpered at his heels. As an afterthought, he grabbed a pair of sunglasses with the leash. *Self defense.*

People streamed in and out of the house two doors down, entering with boxes from the lopsided stacks towering by the door and exiting with the same boxes filled to overflowing. The stacks threatened to topple over every time a box was removed, due to the enthusiasm of the customers.

A woman sat on the porch, surveying the activity. She was flanked by a golden retriever and a schnauzer. Viola whuffed hello to Honey and Chewy, causing Lia to look around, smiling.

"Isn't this wonderful?" she asked Peter as he plopped down in the chair next to hers.

"I've never seen such an organized ring of burglars," Peter said. "I never knew you were a criminal mastermind."

"Smarty. Alma's inside with Jim. Bailey and Jose are with them."

"What the heck is this?"

She pointed to a sign on the lawn declaring "Everything Free."

"When did you come up with this?"

"You've been so busy catching up on case files. I had a chat with Alma about the house last week. I knew she could get so much more for the property if it was cleared out. She didn't want the hassle, so I suggested letting people take what they wanted for free in order to empty the house. She and Jim are inspecting the contents as they are uncovered, just to ensure Ruth didn't hide a collection of Tiffany eggs in with the Tupperware."

"I had a look at the inside last month. You're more likely to have the Ark of the Covenant stashed in there."

Lia nodded at a construction dumpster sitting at the curb. "Bailey and Jose are hauling out trash. I bet they wouldn't mind some help."

"What's the pay?"

"Pennies in Heaven."

Peter sat back, arms folded. "Seriously?"

"This *is* for Alma."

"I don't see you hauling trash."

"It *was* my idea. We've only be at this since eight, and the house is half-empty already."

"You're doing a good thing here."

"This place is so lovely. All that leaded glass, the turrets, and the sunroom out back. The light is terrific."

"It does have good bones. Foundation is solid."

"You know, I've been thinking."

"And?"

"I love this house, I'd buy it, but I need a tenant."

"Really?"

"I could make a really good deal on rent if someone would help me with maintenance."

"Thinking about asking Jose?"

"Are you going to make me spell it out?"

"Spell what out?"

"Helena Bonham Carter and Tim Burton. They were a couple. Did you know that?"

"You reading 'Us' these days?"

"I should be that bored. Anyway, they were together for 13 years, but they never lived in the same house. They lived next door to each other. Like a duplex, I think."

"That so?"

"So I was wondering ..."

Peter waited her out.

"How much do you know about home maintenance?"

"I've been known to change a furnace filter or two. Why do you ask?"

"Geezlepete! Do you want to share the house with me or not?"

"Oh? Were you asking?"

Lia punched him in the shoulder.

"Ow! That depends. Do I get the upstairs or the downstairs?"

"Upstairs."

"I'd feel better if you were on the second floor. Second floor is always safer."

"Take it or leave it, Kentucky Boy."

"And those side lights are a security risk. Anyone could smash one and open the front door from the inside. They need to be removed."

"Not on your life. I'll stick a pair of cactuses behind them."

"Not enough light for cactus."

"I'll make fake ones, but the sidelights stay. See, this is what I mean. Conflict."

"I thought we were engaging in creative negotiation."

"If I had a tenant who was just a tenant, they'd have no business telling me what floor to live on or what I need to do to my sidelights."

"How much fun would that be? Would you settle for a security system with glass sensors and a double-cylinder deadbolt?"

"I might. I don't know if we need the alarm system. We have dogs."

"Well then."

"Dourson?"

"Yes, Babe?"

"First glimmer of plumber's crack, and I'm booting your ass out."

"I can live with that."

Chewy's Song

Let's go for a walk
I don't mean a stroll.
I'll pull on my leash
And mark on the trees.

I'll bark at a squirrel
And sniff at some poo.
I'll pee on some tires
And kiss babies, too.

Let's go for a walk.
Let's go for a walk.
Let's go for a walk.
I want a walk!

Author's Notes

SCOOP is real, as are their 88 occupants. I was privileged to tour their sanctuary, and am amazed at the quality of care these special needs cats receive, funded by garage sales, the occasional fund-raiser and Sarah's knitting. Soon they will have a live feed in one of their rooms, so you can spend time with the cats as well. If you would like to learn more about the work SCOOP does with the feral cat population, go to http://www.scoop.org or follow them on facebook, http://ww.facebook.com/scoopcats/.

In 2002, a cow jumped a six-foot fence at a slaughterhouse in Camp Washington, fleeing to Mount Storm Park, which abuts District Five. It eluded capture for 11 days, though there were many reported sightings (later, a rumor spread that a couple who lived adjacent to Mount Storm gave her sanctuary). The cow's escapades received international attention. Peter Max donated $18,000 in paintings to the SPCA in exchange for custody of the cow, whom he named Cincinnati Freedom. Cincinnati Freedom lived out her days in a sanctuary in New York.

I refer to "pony kegs" in Bailey's report of her search for Leroy in Chapter Six. These are a dying breed of mom and pop corner grocery store that can still be found in older neighborhoods. Pony keg refers to the small beer kegs that were once sold in these stores.

Ricard Lopez was an American artist/pest control officer obsessed with Icelandic singer Bjork. Upset by her relationship with another musician, he decided to kill her and commit suicide so they would be in the afterlife together. He sent her an acid letter bomb. Then he shot himself while videotaping the event, complete with an explanation of his motives. He left behind a nine-month video diary of his obsession. Authorities were able to intercept the letter bomb.

During his presidency, Bill Clinton had an affair with White House intern, Monica Lewinsky. Clinton's denial of the affair became the basis for his impeachment trial. Monica's possession of a dress stained with presidential bodily fluids was a critical issue during the proceeds.

A photograph of two-year-old Quincy Kroner meeting his biggest heroes, the neighborhood garbage men, created a brief internet sensation in 2015.

Acknowledgments

Thanks to Sarah Schellenger and the ladies of Knot Only Knitting, for many hours of delightful companionship, and for letting me use them as the basis for this book. Ditto to SCOOP and their inspiring work. Apologies to Sarah for not using her suggested music for the funeral. I just couldn't write Queen into such a solemn event.

To my extensive editorial team: K. e. Neal, my editor; a plethora of volunteer beta readers, who are too numerous to name and whose efforts stunned me; and to She Who Refuses To Be Named, who, as always, is my last arbiter of proper English.

To my compatriots at The Retreat. I love taking this ride with you. Thanks to Russell Blake, George Wier and Nick Russell for allowing me to poke fun at them.

To Elizabeth Mackey, my amazing cover artist.

And lastly, to the morning crew at the dog park, for continual inspiration.

About the Author

Carol Ann Newsome is a writer and painter who lives in Cincinnati with two former street urchins named Shadda and Chewy, and a furry piranha named Gypsy. She and her tribe can be found every morning at the Mount Airy Dog Park.

Books by C. A. Newsome

A Shot in the Bark
Drool Baby
Maximum Security
Sneak Thief
Muddy Mouth
Fur Boys (2017)

Carol loves to hear from readers. You can contact her at carolannnewsome@netzero.net . Join Carol's mailing list at CANewsome.com if you would like to be notified about future releases in the Lia Anderson Dog Park Mysteries series.

CPSIA information can be obtained
at www.ICGtesting.com
Printed in the USA
LVOW13s1448170317

527610LV00010B/857/P